Home With My Heart

A Southland Romance

The Prequel

By Meda White

Home With My Heart
Copyright © 2016 Meda White

Editor: Andrea Grimm Dickinson
Cover Artist: Kari Ayasha, Cover to Cover Designs

Warning: All rights reserved. The unauthorized reproduction or distribution of this copyrighted work is illegal. Criminal copyright infringement, including infringement without monetary gain, is investigated by the FBI and is punishable by up to 5 years in federal prison and a fine of $250,000.

This is a work of fiction. Names, characters, places and occurrences are a product of the author's imagination. Any resemblance to actual persons, living or dead, places or occurrences, is purely coincidental.

All rights reserved.
ISBN: 194128714X
ISBN-13: 978-1-941287-14-9

DEDICATION

To Abba, who makes me capable, creative and complete.

ACKNOWLEDGMENTS

Thank you to those who share dreams, visions, prophecies, and interpretations.

"Every good and perfect gift is from above…"
James 1:17

Chapter One

Dixie Johnson couldn't believe she'd let her sister talk her into a night out at the Whiskey Barrel, a juke in the backwoods of Georgia where all the men might have a set of teeth between them. She tended to notice that sort of thing since one of her jobs was as a dental assistant.

From her position at the bar, she closed her eyes and inhaled the scents of booze and cigarette smoke with a touch of sawdust. She didn't mind the sawdust. Or the booze for that matter. But she'd quit smoking years before, so she could do without the temptation.

"I bet I know what you're thinking." Nancy nudged her.

Dixie opened one eye and peered at her sister. "You got a smoke?"

Nancy chuckled. "Remember when we used to pick up Daddy's cigarettes off the ground after he'd tossed 'em?"

Dixie shook her head. "Those filterless beasts could've killed us."

"Nearly did when Mama caught us."

Dixie could almost still feel the sting of the switch on the backs of her legs. "Daddy just tried not to laugh when Mama told on us."

The bartender approached, and Nancy did the honors of ordering their first round.

If it weren't for the prospect of a better job on the horizon, Dixie would've stayed home with her three daughters. With the hours she'd been keeping since her husband killed himself drunk driving, she didn't get to see them enough, having had to take on a second job to make up for his lost income. It was a sad comment on the former state of their marriage that the only thing she missed about him was his paycheck.

She let out a long breath, wondering again where it had all gone wrong.

Sometimes, she wondered if their intimacy before marriage had led to boredom in the bedroom once they were hitched. The last time they'd had sex was when their youngest daughter had been conceived more than seven years earlier.

The thought of sex reminded her she'd been taking care of herself for way too long. As she looked around the Barrel, she searched for a man who could take on the responsibility, if only for a night. He had to have at least his front teeth though.

She had standards, by golly.

Her cheeks warmed, and she chuckled at herself, knowing it'd never happen. She'd been a teenager when free love reigned, but even so, she hadn't been particularly free about it. She preferred a little affection and a modicum of compatibility.

But here it was 1984, and more women were going after what they wanted, personally and professionally. Was it time for her to join the revolution?

Her gaze swept the bar and stopped at the door. "Hello, Mister Tall, Dark, and…"

Yes. A flash of pearly white showed behind his upturned lips. "Toothy." *Sexy.*

"What are you saying?" Nancy yelled. "I can't hear a thing over this music."

"Nothing," Dixie mouthed as her eyes followed the handsome stranger.

Moving like a man who knew what he wanted, he made a beeline for the cigarette machine. He wore a western shirt tucked into belted jeans and cowboy boots. One of her innocent girlhood dreams had been to marry a cowboy.

Her skin tingled with excitement, and she forced herself to look away.

"Here you go, D." Nancy slid a shot glass and a beer to her. "Wait here. I'll go find my man and your new boss."

Nancy's man of the hour was a farmer who made a good living in corn and cotton. Dixie's hopefully new boss was a friend of his, who was looking to hire a nurse to expand his home health business.

She had a bachelor's degree in nursing and had been working nights as a charge nurse for the last decade. The idea of home healthcare appealed to her because she'd cared for her father at home when he'd been ill.

There was a demand which needed to be met. An untapped market. These were all things she planned to share with Mr. Baker, if they were able to talk over the brouhaha.

The informal *business* meeting was Nancy's idea, but there were moments when Dixie felt it might be a set up. Like when Nancy had chosen Dixie's outfit, reminding Dixie she was going to a bar, not an office. No Sunday dresses.

It was the reason Dixie currently looked as if she'd walked off the set of *Urban Cowboy*. She could've been Debra Winger's body double.

Maybe her potential employer wouldn't notice she'd left her bra at home, and instead, he'd listen to her business ideas. Perhaps Nancy was hoping he'd notice the absence of the undergarment and hire Dixie on the spot. If he was anything like she imagined, based on the businessmen she knew, he'd be buttoned up with white hair and a fat wallet.

Hard to picture a suit in a dive bar.

Dixie tossed the tequila back and enjoyed the burn trailing down her throat to her empty stomach. She was smart, but she was also a woman who never got to let her hair down.

A thrill scorched through her at the thought of being untamed for one night only. If the guy with the teeth was interested, she could possibly get crazy before she had to talk shop. But she'd need more alcohol to pull it off.

When she could breathe again, she slammed the shot glass on the bar and got the bartender's attention. "Another, please."

***

It seemed like a hundred years since Dan Baker had seen the inside of a country bar. Walking into the place, he'd been assaulted by noise and enticed by cigarette smoke. A band played, and the people spoke loudly, so they could be heard above the ruckus.

He'd given up smoking for his wife, but tonight, he sought comfort in the soothing vapor of an old friend. He selected his brand of choice from the machine near the jukebox and checked for flammable objects, like fashionable ladies with big hair, before he struck the flint in his lighter.

He didn't want to be responsible for setting the hair afire of one of the lovelies who'd spent so much time teasing and taming their coiffure.

A memory of his wife's bald head punched him in the gut.

With the first drag, he knew it was a mistake.

The delicious taste on his tongue gave way to a lung-filling, emotion-soothing euphoria. He'd missed his old friend Winston. There would be no coming back from this walk on the wild side.

The only thing that might taste better than Winston was the long-legged redhead at the bar. As he approached, she turned and ran right into him.

His arms instinctively closed around her. "Whoa there, darlin'. If you needed a hug, all you had to do was ask."

Her mouth hung open a full second before her luscious lips turned up into a heart-stopping smile. "So, hugs are free?"

"Yeah." He smirked. "And your next drink can

be too. Can I get you another?"

"This one's nearly full." She raised her beer bottle.

"That doesn't mean you can't have another." He stared too long into her brilliant blue eyes.

She seemed to consider before she answered. "All right. One more shot of tequila will set me up for the rest of the night."

"One more?" He raised a brow and let his gaze drift down her body. *Hot damn.* He'd been a widower too long. "Well, it's yours then, darlin'. Don't go away."

He stepped past her to the bar and ordered two shots. Turning back, he asked, "Do you need salt and lemon to go with that?"

"Nah. That stuff's for sissies." She shot him a slow wink, which sent a rush of heat though his veins faster than white lightning.

It might have been a combination of the smoke and the atmosphere, but a woman hadn't turned his head in a year and a half. The vibe in the air told him anything could happen. If he was going to rejoin the land of the living, tonight seemed like a good time to do it. And this auburn-haired beauty seemed like the one to do it with.

He handed her the liquor and held his up for a toast. For a second, he wished he was in the habit of charming women with words. A smooth line might make her ask for a hug for real.

All that came to his mind was an old Indian proverb he'd learned as a child, so he blurted it out. "All dreams spin out from the same web."

Her eyes widened as her brows rose slowly. A

moment later, one corner of her gorgeous mouth tipped up. "Here's to dreams."

They clinked glasses and tossed the liquid fire down their throats.

Dan contained his shudder, but enjoyed every millisecond of hers.

He turned back to the bar and grabbed the beer he'd ordered, using the time to calm himself down. After a long pull, he reached for his wallet and paid the bartender.

By the time that was done, he could face the beautiful woman.

Eyes. Look her in the eyes.

Her head was tipped back as she drained her beer. He clenched his fist to keep a finger from tracing the soft line of her exposed neck.

Damn. His body reacted again.

Football. Baseball. Wrestling. Dancing. Wait. "Would you care to dance?"

Setting their bottles on the bar, he held out his hand and she took it, following him onto the dance floor. He two-stepped her around to a Ronnie Milsap tune until the band slowed it down with "We've Got Tonight" by Kenny Rogers and Sheena Easton. Someone must be trying to tell him something.

It had been too long since a woman's hips swayed in his hands. How he longed for a dance without pants, but he kept his mouth shut. The likelihood of getting slapped was high.

She felt so right in his arms with her chest pressed against him and her temple resting against his cheek. He couldn't pass up the chance to see if she might be willing to explore the scorching inferno between them.

    He put out a feeler. "I just got a new Blazer."

    "Hmm." Her breath was hot on his neck. "I think I'd like to see that."

Chapter Two

Dixie let the man take her hand and lead her out to his new sport utility vehicle. He said he'd gotten it so he could go off-roading, and then he spoke of cylinders and torque. Dixie didn't know what he was talking about, but she relished the deep timbre of his voice. His accent was thick like molasses, and she imagined his lips close to her ear saying provocative things in the dark of night.

"What exactly do you mean by off-roading?" She batted her lashes, something she'd rarely done before, but she had only one thing on her mind.

"You know, take it out in a field and try to get it stuck. This baby has four-wheel drive, so it can get out of most anywhere."

It had rained scads the day before, and the dirt road leading to the Whiskey Barrel had been treacherous in her sister's Volvo.

"You'll have to show me, or I won't believe it." Dixie thought she had a feel for this man after only an hour of talking and dancing with him, and sure enough, the challenge got her the desired result.

"Climb on in, darlin'."

She was already leaning into the driver's door, so she got in with a little assistance in the form of his hand on her rear end. Keeping her denim mini skirt over her backside was nearly impossible as she crossed the console to the passenger seat. She hoped the big guy got an eyeful.

She was happy to note there was a bench seat in the back.

He slid behind the wheel and cranked the engine. "Let's go get this thing stuck."

If her brain hadn't been dulled by alcohol, she might have seen the folly in their plan. As it was, she wanted to get stuck in a remote place with this good lookin' man and see if he could get her motor running.

"A friend of mine has a farm nearby," he said. "I'll take you in one of his fields and show you a good time."

"I hope so." She cut her gaze to catch him watching the road with one eye and her with the other.

It was convenient that Big D, as he told her to call him, had a cooler of beer in the back. She climbed over the console to get herself a drink. Judging by his inability to concentrate on the road, he was enjoying the peekaboo show she played with her little skirt.

They slipped and slid around the field, flinging mud all over the vehicle. Big D even let her drive, and there had been a near kiss when they'd exchanged seats.

There had been a real, hot kiss when they changed back.

Dixie put her hand on his knee, willing herself to move it up his thigh, but she hesitated, which made him slow things down.

"Are you ready to get back?" he asked after breaking the kiss.

"Not really. I'm having fun with you."

He put it in drive and hit the accelerator, only to find they were going nowhere. She was glad he'd been the last one to do the doughnut or else he might blame her.

"Something wrong?" she asked.

"Maybe not, let me get out and have a look."

While he checked the tires, she slipped her panties off and put them her purse.

He climbed back in. "Well, we appear to be stuck. We can drink some more beer and pass the time, or you can wait here while I walk to my buddy's house and get his tractor."

"Sounds good."

"What?"

"Passing the time." Not wearing underwear gave her more confidence.

Her mother would roll over in her grave, but tonight, Dixie was going to have some of that free love she'd been missing out on.

She leaned across the console and kissed Big D just enough to tease him. Then she bolted for the back seat.

***

Flooded. Dixie overflowed with every sensation of pleasure. She waited, knowing the elation would recede.

She caught her breath while her denim skirt, bunched at her waist along with her tank top, dug into her mid-back as she lay on the bench seat. She observed a bead of condensation roll down the window above her head. *Steamy*.

Big D sat up then helped her straighten her clothes before she snuggled next to him, his arm around her shoulders. With his free hand, he lit them each a cigarette.

Hesitantly, she took it. There was really only one habit she wanted to get back into, and it wasn't smoking.

"I hope this doesn't chap your behind, but you never told me your name," he said.

She exhaled a cloud of smoke. "You can keep calling me darlin'. Or D if you prefer."

"D, as in Donna?"

"Tell me what your D stands for, and I'll tell you mine."

"Well, darlin', isn't it obvious?" A slight smirk landed on his lips.

So, the man knew he was blessed. It figured a guy who seemed nice and showed promise would be just what his initial indicated—with a capital D.

Studying the planes of his face, she tried to decide if he was confident or arrogant.

Fighting disappointment, she took a swig of beer. "I'm ready to take that walk to your friend's house now."

***

What in the heck had Dan done to tick her off? Must've been the name thing. Clearly, she didn't want him to know hers, but then it'd been his dumb idea to offer only his initial. It would've been nice to hear her call his name when they'd been intimate.

"I'll go," he said. "The mud's ankle deep. Your little red boots will get dirty. Just relax, finish your beer, and I'll be back soon."

"Wait." She gripped his forearm and bit her lower lip.

The woman who flirted fearlessly and wore no drawers now seemed shy and uncertain. The flash of wariness in her eyes awakened his protective instincts.

He took her hand and held it. "What is it, darlin'?"

She looked down and shook her head. "I'm sorry. It's silly. It's nothing."

"Whatever it is, you can tell me."

"It's really nothing." She made eye contact again. "I just got scared about waiting out here by myself. I'll be fine though. No one even knows we're here."

"Don't worry. Nobody's gonna bother you." He paused as his chest tightened. "You're not afraid of *me*, are you?"

Her smile lit up the dark. "Are you kidding? After what we just did?" She sighed. "Maybe you should be afraid of me."

"Oh, yeah?" He leaned in and tickled her ribs.

Giggling, she squirmed until his mouth met hers. Then she molded herself to him.

This woman was going to be his undoing. It was possible she'd manipulated him, but it was what he'd wanted, so he'd gone along every step of the way.

He didn't want to get unstuck. Not for a long while. If he could stay in the backseat of this truck, happily making whoopee with his mysterious new lady, he'd do it.

His wife would be terribly disappointed in him.

The thought reminded him of his boys. He'd at least need to be home when they woke up in the morning.

What happened between now and then was totally up to D.

"D," he rasped in her ear. "I will eventually take that walk, but since we're here, I wondered if—"

"Yes," she said.

"I get the feeling you've been neglected, little lady. I'm gonna take care of you." He slid his hand under her skirt. "I'm so glad you forgot the undies."

She pressed her lips together. "They're in my purse."

A laugh started deep in his belly and shook them both. "Not quite the vixen after all, huh?"

"Sorry, but no."

"Don't apologize. I'm not the hound dog I appear to be either."

It was her turn to chuckle. The sound lightened his heart.

Taking it slowly, he peeled off every inch of her clothes, even though they were few. And for the first time in a long time, he made love to a woman.

Chapter Three

Definitely not a prick.
When they'd heard the telltale sound of a tractor approaching, Big D had helped Dixie get dressed before he did, even making sure her tank top was on right side out.

She grinned as he climbed to the front seat, put his boots on, and got out to greet his friend. Trying to minimize her movements, she slid into the front passenger seat and cracked open the completely fogged window to allow fresh air in and some of their heat to escape.

Part of her was glad for the interruption. If they'd kept going at it all night, she'd be bowlegged by tomorrow.

And crap. She had to get back to the bar to meet Dan Baker.

Her cheeks were still heated from what she'd just done and from almost getting caught. But she supposed if she was going to do the backseat bump like a teenager in a borrowed field, she'd have to accept the risk that went with it. It was a good thing she lived thirty miles away.

The tractor moved in front of the Blazer. Then the owner switched it off while he and Big D messed around with ropes or chains or something.

With one hand covering her face, Dixie hunched down in the seat.

"Who you got steaming up those windows?" the tractor owner asked.

"No one you know." Big D's voice was firm.

"It's probably nobody you know either. Ella would be ashamed."

Dixie's breath stuck in her throat.

"That's why I'm glad she won't find out," Big D said. "No one will. Right, Bud?"

"Your secret's safe with me," the guy said.

Married. The son of a gun was married.

She'd been out of the dating scene so long it hadn't occurred to her that a married man might be out on the prowl.

With the palm she'd used to shade her face, she smacked her forehead. She was a Blue Ribbon Idiot.

Had she ever thrown herself at a man before? Not that she could remember, but the first one she aimed for, she got. Landed right on top of his big married—

It took every bit of restraint she had to subdue a primal scream begging to rip from her throat.

Why? Why did she have to be such a fool?

The tractor engine roared to life, and a moment later, Big D got behind the wheel of the Blazer. She ground her teeth and looked out the window, still blurred with condensation.

Moments later, they were pulled free of their ruts, and Big D slammed the shifter from neutral to park before he got out to unhook and thank his friend.

Once back inside, he put his hand on her knee. "Where to, darlin'?"

"I need to get back to the Barrel." She glanced his way and tried to disguise the tightness in her voice with a small smile. Though she should cuss him out and cut his balls off, she'd rather pretend she didn't know the truth and wasn't hurt by it.

"You have somebody waiting for you there?" He hesitated, clearly hoping they'd have another round of the four-legged fox trot.

"I hope so. I didn't tell my sister I was leaving. She's probably worried sick." *Yeah, that's it. Blame Nancy. Good thinking, D.*

"Maybe she's having just as good a time."

Dixie plastered a fake smile on her face. "Oh, I have no doubt she's having a blast, but she'll still notice my absence. Nancy's a multitasker."

"Your sister's named Nancy?" His brow furrowed.

She felt herself mirroring his expression. "Yeah."

"Damn." He managed to make it a two syllable word.

Good. He'd probably heard of Nancy and knew she was a lawyer. She might even know his wife.

Ha-ha. Serves you right, jackass. Dixie turned her smirk away from Big D and reveled in her smugness. Nancy wouldn't tell, and the last thing

Dixie wanted was to break up a marriage, but the two-timer could sweat it out indefinitely for all she cared.

***

If he wasn't mistaken, Dan had just dipped his pen in the company ink, so to speak. If this woman was the one he hoped to hire to launch a new business venture, he'd screwed up royally.

He didn't have the heart to ask if her name was Dixie, but then, he already knew the answer. Pinching the bridge of his nose between his thumb and forefinger, he shook his head. He should admit it, apologize, and move on. But the truth was, he wasn't a darn bit sorry.

Unable to figure out what to say without sounding callous, he bit his tongue.

They drove in silence the rest of the way to the Barrel. Her easy-going, up-for-anything façade had been replaced by a mask of solemnity, making him wonder if she'd figured it out too.

Almost as soon as he hit the parking lot, she bolted out of his Blazer, and he had to employ his full stride to keep up. He caught her at the door to the bar and put his hand on her back. The place was packed, and he wondered if they'd even be able to get inside to find her sister.

One second his hand was on her. The next she ducked under a man's arm as he put it around a woman, squeezing between them.

D popped up on the other side and kept moving. Dan walked around the couple, but once he was past them, she was nowhere to be seen.

He nudged his way to the bar, hoping to catch a

glimpse of her.

A fleshy woman he knew took him by surprise and wrapped her arms around him. Her cleavage threatened to spill out of her low cut top, but she didn't hold half the appeal of the woman he'd just taken for a ride.

"It's so good to see you out and about, Dan. Ella would be so happy you're living again. Did you know I got divorced? I'd love to make you dinner sometime. Call me, okay?" Reba took a pen out of her purse and wrote her number on the palm of his hand.

He let her because he had nowhere to run in this sardine can.

Reba had been on the PTA with his late wife. The fact she'd announced her divorce and invited him to dinner in the same breath turned him way off.

He scanned the bar and spotted his redhead in the back corner. Sure enough, his buddy Brent and his lady friend Nancy were seated at the table.

Pushing through the throng of people, he detoured to the side wall, hoping to find a path. By the time he got to the table, D was gone.

"There you are," Brent said. "We wondered if you were gonna leave us hanging, Big Dan. You just missed Nancy's sister. She's not feeling well, so she's leaving."

Nancy stood. "I'll see if I can catch her."

"Don't bother," Dan said. "I don't think she'll be very happy to be introduced to me."

"Nonsense. She'd be perfect for your business enterprise, and the poor thing needs a break from the schedule she's currently keeping." Nancy started to walk away.

Dan caught her arm. "Dixie and I are already acquainted. We bumped into each other at the bar." *And other things in my backseat.*

"I hope you didn't talk shop the whole time." Brent winked.

"We didn't." Dan slid into a chair and lit a cigarette. *And now we never will.*

***

Dixie answered the phone early the next morning, hoping the girls wouldn't hear it and could sleep in.

"I'm happy to report I made it home safely and shagged rotten," Nancy said.

"Sister, there are some things I just don't need to know." Dixie laughed.

"Uh-huh. And you never told me where you disappeared to last night."

Dixie debated how much to tell, but they shared almost everything with each other. Since she didn't know the guy's real name, she decided to spill some of the beans. "I was a bad girl."

Then she chickened out and changed the subject. "Whatever happened to Brent's friend? The one with the job?"

"He was there," Nancy said. "He told us you met and talked."

"No. I left with a guy, for a little while, so I never met Brent's friend."

"Who was the guy?" Nancy's voice revealed the wriggle that must've been happening with her eyebrows.

"I think his name was Dick, as in Richard—"

"You think?" Nancy giggled. "Sister, you *were* a bad girl."

"I never told him my full name either, so D and Big D had a little romp." Dixie smiled to herself.

"What did you call him?"

"Big D, and he wasn't lying about that either."

"Um, Sister, I hate to tell you this, but the man with the job is known to his friends as Big Dan, or Big D if they're lazy. You may have just slept your way into a new job. I hope he liked it. Better yet, I hope you did."

"Dammit, Nancy, stop messing with me." Heat flushed through her right before a boulder landed hard in the pit of her stomach.

She covered her eyes with her pillow. "You know how much I need that job, but you also know I can't work for someone I've slept with. Especially, when he's married."

"He's married? No way. I don't know him very well, but I don't believe it."

"Believe it. His wife's name is Ella. I found out after the fact. What happened to fidelity?" Her limbs felt heavy. "Where did all the good men go?"

"Well, his loss, your gain, little sister. You don't want to work for a creep like him anyway. I would call Brent and give him a piece of my mind, but I guess it's not his fault his friend's a louse."

"Don't say anything to Brent. I don't want anyone to know I had a single serving with a married man. Well, a double serving. Promise me, Nancy."

"I promise, but I'm just so surprised. Dan

seemed like a nice guy."

"Yeah, he fooled me too. Don't get me wrong. He was nice to look at and fun, but I guess he likes having his cake and all that jazz. If he said he talked to me, he must've figured out who I was at some point."

"And he didn't come clean with you? The jackass. He should've had the decency to admit it to you. But if he was lying about his marital status, I guess that's to be expected." Nancy's tone took on the same pinched, nasal-like quality their mother's had when she'd been unhappy.

"I think you're more upset than I am. What gives?" Dixie appreciated her sister getting indignant on her behalf, but it felt like there was more to it.

"It's just...I thought this job was the answer. I see you running yourself into the ground taking care of your girls. You're not eating. You're not sleeping—"

"Hey, they're my priority, and things will be better once I pay off Steve's debts. Besides, the one time I do something for me, look what happened."

"I wish you'd let Brother and me help you more."

"Sister, Larry has already employed me, and your daughter babysits my kids for free. You do help me. You're a single mom, too. I'll earn my way for my girls and me, but I won't do it on my back."

Chapter Four

Dan propped his elbows on his desk and rubbed his eyes. It had been an agonizing month at work. Normally, he loved his job, but his new business idea kept running into brick walls or rather brick women.

As the owner of a chain of home health supply stores, he was the boss and he was good at it. His vision to make the company something more was etched into his soul, and he couldn't let it go without a fight.

During the end stages of Ella's battle with breast cancer, she'd wanted to be at home but had to be put in a facility to keep her comfortable. He'd gotten the visiting nurses idea and thought to expand his business to serve a need. His initial research indicated it could be profitable.

Some people wanted to die at home surrounded by their loved ones. If he could afford to give that as a gift to everyone, he would.

He still planned to offer services on payment plans and a sliding scale to those without insurance and to whom it would be a financial burden. He'd most likely write some of them off in the end. Since he'd married money and had also become a self-made millionaire, he had the means to assist a lot of people.

As a father, one of his goals was to teach his sons the value of a dollar, so they'd be smart enough in managing their finances to always have extra to help those in need.

He'd poured over résumés, endured countless interviews, and hired and fired two different nurses, only to learn they were all Nurse Ratched.

Pushing back from his workspace, his hand hit a stack of papers, knocking them across his desk and some onto the floor. "Damn it all."

When he bent down to get them, he noticed a scrap of paper under his chair. Without thought, he tossed it in the trash.

A glimpse of the paper put him on his knees, his face in the wastebasket. He pulled the scrap out triumphantly and read the name aloud, "Dixie Jensen Johnson, Registered Nurse."

He hadn't stopped thinking about her and their night together in the bog. Just the memory excited him, until he remembered how quickly she'd run off.

Even though she'd probably never talk to him, he needed to get her number and see if there was a chance she'd work with him. An acquaintance had told him how Dixie had been there for his dying father in the ICU. When Dan had heard about her from another friend, he'd known in his gut Dixie was the one he needed.

He pressed the intercom button on his fancy work phone. "Betty Jo, I need a telephone book."

His secretary came into his office and plopped the book onto his desk. "Anything else, boss?"

"Is there fresh coffee?"

"Do you know who you're talking to? Of course, there is." She started out the door. "I guess I can bring you a cup."

She was a little sassy for Dan's taste, but she did a good job, and she'd picked up the slack when he'd taken time off to be with Ella. Betty Jo was good people, and he needed more like her on staff.

He flipped through the white pages and ran his finger down the page of J's.

Johnson, D. Must be it.

Before he could talk himself out of it, he dialed the number.

"Johnson residence," a woman's voice answered.

"Ah, hi. Hello. Dixie?"

"Dixie is unavailable. May I take a message?" The voice was clipped and crisp.

"Who am I speaking with?"

"Who's calling?" More of that sass women liked to use to put a man in his place.

"This is Dan Baker. I'm trying to reach Dixie about a job."

"A job? She already has two and doesn't need another. We can't spare her, but thank you for calling. Good—"

"Wait, Miss. Would you please take my

number and ask Dixie to call me?"

There was a pause. "Okay. Go ahead, Mr. Baker."

Silently, he exhaled before he gave the number. "What's your name, Miss? So I know who to thank."

"This is Liz."

"Well, thank you, Liz, honey." He hung up the phone and spoke aloud. "Who the hell is Liz?"

He dropped his head into his hands and prayed Dixie would give him a chance.

***

Dixie wadded the paper and tossed the note in the kitchen trash. There was no way she could return the call.

She hadn't seen him in a month, but his face and every other part of him were still firmly fixed in her mind. He hadn't even left her alone in her dreams, making the few hours of sleep she tried to get impossible.

"Mama, why'd you throw it away? What kind of job does that man want to talk to you about?" The almond-shaped eyes of her eldest daughter assessed her.

"It's nothing, Lizabelle. Thanks for being my little grown-up and taking the message. If he calls back, tell him I'm not interested." Dixie opened the pantry and stared at the meager offerings.

"Okay, Mama. Is he a bad man?"

"No, baby, nothing like that." She wanted her girls to be cautious but not fearful. "He's just not someone I want to work with. On second thought, I'll call him, so he won't bother us again."

Dixie reached into the trash can and retrieved the note written in Liz's precise handwriting.

She checked the clock. It was a few minutes before five in the evening. She needed to get dinner ready, feed the girls, make sure their homework was done, and get to work by 10:30.

"I'll start dinner, Mama." Liz gave her a little push toward the phone hanging on the kitchen wall.

Dixie grunted as she picked up the receiver, dread filling her.

"Home Health, Dan Baker's office," a female voice answered.

"Hey, there." *Gosh, she sounded like a hick.*

But if she remembered correctly, and she did, Big Dan Baker had sounded the same with his thick Southern drawl.

"Uh, this is Dixie Johnson returning Mr. Baker's call. Is he available?"

"I'm sorry, ma'am. He left a few minutes early to get to the boys' baseball games. Can I take your name and number?"

"Actually, I'll leave my name and a message... Tell Mr. Baker not to call Dixie Johnson again. Thank you." She put the receiver down, telling herself she was being firm, not rude.

An odd sense of unease crept up her spine, and she darted her gaze side to side looking for the cause. Seeing nothing, a feeling settled on her like she'd just let an opportunity pass by.

She'd been having odd sensations and seeing unusual things since childhood. When the signals were clear, she could brace herself for what came next. When they were signs she'd learned to interpret, she dealt with it as best as possible. But when it was something inexplicable, it scared her to death.

Shaking it off, she took over dinner preparation, and Liz picked up her daddy's old electric guitar and played something, which almost sounded like music. Dixie wished she could afford to get lessons for Liz, but with the current balance of her checking account, there was nothing to spare.

Tuning out the noise, Dixie was deep in thought when the phone rang.

Liz, who'd designated herself as the telephone operator, held out the receiver. "Mama, it's Aunt Nancy."

Dixie took the phone. "Hey, Sister."

"I found something out and think you should know."

"Does it have to do with a certain Mr. Dan Baker? If so, I don't want to hear it." She stretched the telephone cord across the counter and stirred the bright orange macaroni and cheese with renewed vigor.

"Okay, I won't tell you, but if he calls, I think you should give him a chance."

"No way, José. It's too late anyway. I basically told him to buzz off."

"All right then. Have it your way," Nancy said. "How are my nieces?"

"Growing every time I blink my eyes. Katie wants to be in another beauty pageant. I had to tell her no because I can't afford it. She wants to get some babysitting jobs like Liz to make money, so she can pay the entry fee and buy a dress, but she's too young to babysit on her own."

"Are you sure you don't want to talk to Dan Baker?"

"I have my pride, Nancy," she said, trying to invoke the same firm tone she'd used with the lady at Dan Baker's office.

"Be sure that pride doesn't deprive your girls of opportunities. Those pageants Katie loves so much can provide a lot of scholarship money. Can you say *college fund*? Not to mention, have you ever heard of a Miss America who wasn't successful in life? Those girls are driven, just like your Katie."

A little while later, as the girls ate, Dixie sat at the table with them and rubbed the folded piece of paper between her fingers.

"Mama, aren't you gonna eat?" Maddie asked.

"I'm just waiting to make sure you've had enough, little one."

"I'm full." Her youngest pushed her half-empty plate away.

"But, you didn't eat very much," Dixie said. "I tell you what. I'll eat a little and save you some for later."

Dixie had grown accustomed to little Maddie's peculiar eating habits. She was a grazer. She wouldn't eat much at one sitting, but an hour or two later, she'd be back, acting like she was starved.

All of her girls were thin, but Maddie was downright bony. The other mothers often commented about it at dance class. Dixie could choose to take it as an insult to her parenting or a compliment to her daughter's metabolism.

Sometimes, she hated doing the parenting thing alone. She was sure God never intended it to be that way, but she'd been left without a lot of options. Having an occasional sounding board would be nice, but she didn't want to unload her personal problems on her patients or co-workers.

Sometimes, in the wee hours of the night, when she'd check on her intensive care patients, she'd sit by them and talk about everything on her heart. Most of them were comatose, and most folks would say they never knew she was there. But it helped to pretend she had someone to talk to, and Dixie knew they could hear, just maybe not with their ears.

When they were near the end and Dixie was on duty, she'd be the last to see them go. Not their physical bodies, but their spirits. It was a gift she'd inherited from her father who was part Hopi and had spent some of his childhood with his grandparents' tribe out west.

The departed would walk past the nurse's station, pause, smile, and wave before they poofed out of sight. She always got the feeling they connected with her. It was probably due to hearing about her problems. They felt they knew her. Or it could be wishful thinking.

Everyone needed someone to connect with.

Dixie widened her eyes to stem the pressure of tears building. She couldn't let her girls know she was lonely. Not for one second did she ever want them to think they weren't enough.

Chapter Five

Dan read and reread the handwritten message Betty Jo had given him from Dixie. Despite all reason, he'd made up his mind he was gonna have Dixie Johnson, one way or another. Employee would probably be the best option, but he could handle both ways. When he was determined, he didn't let anything get in his way.

He gripped the telephone receiver tight in his hand. "Hey, Brent. It's Big Dan. Listen, I need to speak to Nancy about her sister."

After the call, Dan took a deep breath and dialed again. "Nancy, Dan Baker here. I really want to talk to Dixie."

Thankfully, he didn't meet any resistance from Dixie's sister, and she gave him the information he needed.

With a strategy in mind, he stood and shut off the lamp on his desk.

Addressing the framed photo nearby, he said,

"If you're an angel in heaven, and I know you are, I'm gonna need a little help with this one." He pressed two fingers to his lips and touched the glass protecting the image of his late wife.

"Betty Jo, I have to cut out early. Ballgame. See you tomorrow." He breezed out like he owned the place. *Ha.* It was a good thing he did.

Dan pulled up to the Mini-Might's practice field in Bull Creek, one town over from Willow Creek where he lived. He was gonna be late for his boys' baseball games, but since he had to run from field to field to field to see them all anyway, they probably wouldn't notice he was missing for a little while.

He sat in his Blazer for a minute, trying to plan what he would say.

A Chevy Caprice wagon pulled up, leaving a few spaces between his vehicle and theirs, and a buttload of girls piled out. The last one to close the door was a very attractive redhead.

His heart skipped a beat, and he lit a cigarette to buy time as he watched Dixie herd four girls wearing cheer uniforms through the gate. Exhaling a white cloud, he thumped the cigarette away before he followed.

Taking the first entrance, he climbed to the top of the bleachers, so he could have the best vantage point. He wasn't spying. He was gathering intelligence, so he would be better prepared to make his move.

Dixie's fingers were a blur as she braided the hair of three of the girls, one after the other. The weird thing was the hair color. One was pale blonde, almost white, and two were reddish-blonde. None were auburn like their mama. The fourth girl was also blonde but a more medium shade. He wondered if she was Nancy's teenage daughter.

He'd had a nice conversation with Nancy, learning several things about her sister, but not nearly enough. Dixie's husband was deceased, and she lived for her three girls. Nancy had a lot of knowledge about Dixie's work experience as well.

"Listen, you two need to sit down and straighten out your misunderstandings. See if you can reach some kind of agreement," Nancy had said. "My sister's stubborn and prideful, but something has to change. She's killing herself because she wants to give her kids everything."

When the girls abandoned Dixie to take the field in different clumps of cheerleaders, Dan made his move.

"Cute kids." He sat next to her.

Her smile faded when she realized who he was, and she seemed at a loss for words.

"I liked the smile better," he said. "Don't be upset because I tracked you down. I really need to talk to you about a job. Say you'll come into the office to chat, and I'll leave you be. Otherwise, I'll sit here 'til the cows come home."

"I'm sorry, Mr. Baker, but—"

"Dan, please, call me Dan. I mean, you do know me intimately." He suppressed a smirk.

"You just made my case. Thank you, Dan. Now go away before—dammit." She turned her attention to the approaching girl. "Hey, sweetie. What do ya need?"

"Mama, do you have more bobby pins? Shelly's hair's falling, and she's scared she'll get in trouble."

"I sure do, baby." Dixie reached into her purse, which was about the size of his briefcase, maybe bigger. "Here you go, take this whole thing and put it by the fence when you're done. I'll come get it."

"Hey, doll," Dan said to the little blonde girl.

"Hello, I'm Katie." She curtsied.

She was so stinking cute he lost a little piece of his heart. "Dan Baker." He extended his hand.

She shook it, giving him a smile and a nod. "You know my mama?"

Dan opened his mouth to answer in the affirmative, but Dixie cut him off.

"Baby, you better go. Shelly's waiting."

"Okay. Nice to meet you, Dan Baker, I mean, Mr. Dan Baker. Excuse me." She curtsied again and ran off.

"She's adorable and very well-spoken. She's your middle child?"

Dixie looked at him with slightly less of a scowl than she'd previously worn. "Yes. It appears you've been spying."

"I prefer to call it doing my homework. I like to know as much as possible about my employees before they come to work for me."

"There it is again, that confidence that borders on arrogance. It's almost attractive, but not quite. No, thank you, Mr. Baker." Her tone grew more firm.

"See? That's just what I need, honesty from my employees."

"Call me your employee one more time and ensure I never work with you." Her teeth were clenched tight to match her fisted hands.

He put his palms up in a defensive gesture until she relaxed. "So you would consider it? Even after…" In his mind, he pictured her in his backseat.

Baseball, baseball, baseball.

"I promise to never mention what happened or call you my employee, if you'll meet with me. I know you want a better life for your girls and more time to enjoy being with them."

He pulled his business card out of his pocket. He'd already written his home number on the back, just in case. "Call me when you have a minute, so we can set it up. At the office. Strictly professional."

She worked her jaw side to side. "You're manipulative."

"I'm not the only one." He grinned.

She cut her eyes at him. "Strictly professional?"

"You have my word."

"I'm not sure how much that's worth."

She couldn't have injured him worse if she'd slapped him. He took pride in his word. Integrity was a value he practiced and preached.

"I don't know where you get your information, Miss Johnson, but I can assure you my word's something you can count on."

"Would your wife agree with you?"

He narrowed his eyes. "You don't know anything about my wife." It was his turn to speak through clenched teeth.

She pressed her lips together and turned away. "Excuse me." Moving down the bleachers and closer to the field, she left him sitting there with his mouth open.

He'd never been insulted and dismissed in the space of so little time.

Sudden awareness hit him about the misunderstanding Nancy had mentioned.

He wasn't perfect, but he wasn't the callous bastard Dixie thought he was. No matter what it took, he'd make her see who he really was, but he'd work on clearing the air later. For now, he would be the bigger man and leave her in peace. Although, from what he'd learned about her, he had a feeling she hadn't known peace in a long time.

***

After riding in Dixie's purse for a few days, Big Dan Baker's business card was worn out. The number on the back had almost faded because she'd held it in her clammy hands long before she knew it was there. She'd also crumpled it and straightened it a dozen times.

Dan's company was a chance for her to make a better way for her girls. He'd nailed her on that one. Also, he'd just plain nailed her. It wouldn't be so much of a dilemma if he weren't married, but it would still be a slight issue. He was an attractive man. She couldn't help but feel warm inside when he got near.

With that realization, she'd just cracked the real problem wide open. She was afraid of herself, afraid she wouldn't be able to resist him while working in close proximity, wife or not.

She tried to tell herself the wife changed everything, but when she asked herself if she'd give up the hour they'd spent in the back of his truck, she couldn't in all honesty say she would. She'd wanted it and she'd enjoyed it. The memory taunted and teased her more often than she would ever admit.

"Okay, D. It's time to get over yourself. This is honest work no matter how you met your boss. It's for your girls."

The pep talk came courtesy of the catalog the dance teacher had given her for spring recital costumes. She might have to take a loan from her brother or sister after all.

It was almost eight o'clock on Sunday night. If she waited much longer, it would be too late to call.

"Hello."

The deep male voice startled her. She stared at the phone.

Too late to turn back now.

"Um, yes, hello. May I speak to Dan?"

"Speaking. Who's this?"

"Hi, Mr. Baker, this is Dixie…uh, Johnson."

"Hey there, darlin'. I was hoping you'd call me."

She swallowed her ire at being called darlin'. She'd been putting up with pats and pet names from her male superiors for years. At least this one had justification for calling her by a term of endearment. She was just glad his wife hadn't answered.

Dixie was going to hell in a handbasket for sure.

"I'm ready to talk." She let out a sigh of relief after she said it.

"Are you free tomorrow?"

"I get off of my day job a little after noon. I can be at your office by one."

"I'll have lunch for us."

"No, thank you. I'll eat before I get there."

"Suit yourself, darlin'. Oops, forget I called you that. It slipped out by mistake." He paused and silence filled the line. "You doin' okay?"

Her eyes pricked and her throat clogged at the genuine concern in his voice. She had to remind herself who she was talking to.

"Um." She cleared her throat. "Yes, I'm fine. Thank you for asking."

"How 'bout those pretty little girls?"

"All fine, thanks. I'll see you tomorrow at your office. One o'clock." She hung up.

Earlier in the day, her daughters had gotten into an argument over clothes, and some profanity had hit the air waves. She hated to punish them for something she was guilty of herself, but she couldn't let it go.

All three girls got bars of Dove soap in their mouths for a few minutes. Her mama had done the same to her and Nancy and Larry, so she knew it would work, for a little while anyway.

Even more upsetting than her girls fighting was the phone call she'd received before she decided to get in touch with Dan. One of the bill collectors was checking to be sure they would get their payment on time. It wasn't even late yet.

Her shoulders sagged and she shook her head, aggravated by the fact it was Steve's bookie in Atlanta.

She'd known he'd gambled and owed people, but she'd had no idea how much. Sometimes, she wondered if he might have been able to avoid hitting the bull the night he was killed, but she couldn't go there.

She would never utter her theory out loud. Her girls already knew their dad wasn't around like other kids' dads because he drank. They didn't need to know the rest. It was her job to protect them, and she intended to do just that.

She shivered at the offer the bookie had presented as a way she could work off Steve's debt faster. There was no way she would do it on her back, so she'd called Dan, even though being on her back with him had gotten her foot in the door.

At least with him, she had a promise of no future funny business. In her opinion, he was the lesser of two evils. Whether or not he was a man of his word remained to be seen. Any guy who cheated on his wife wasn't very trustworthy in her eyes, but it still beat the bookie's suggestion.

Chapter Six

Dan ordered lunch, despite Dixie's assurance she would eat in advance. She was on the thin side, so if he could ply her with food, she might agree to work with him.

The intercom buzzed. "Mr. Baker, your one o'clock is here."

He checked the time and smiled. She was early.

When Dixie entered his office, she didn't look quite like he'd remembered, and she wasn't dressed for an interview.

He stood and indicated the chair by his desk.

"I'm sorry to be early and in uniform." She sat. "I'm running on fumes."

"No need to apologize. Are you hungry?" He held up a Styrofoam plate with barbeque pork, white bread, and baked beans.

The look on her face said she wanted the food, but her jaw worked as if she was about to say no.

"Here, eat." He placed the plate in front of her

and passed her a set of plastic utensils.

"Thank you." She kept her head down as she worked the cellophane wrapper.

"How early did you get up this morning?"

She regarded him. "I've been up since about four o'clock yesterday afternoon."

"That's what I thought. How would you like to set your own hours? I won't lie. You'll be working a lot before the launch, but you'll be able to sleep at night, watch your girls cheer, and work at home after they go to bed."

She slumped in her chair, and her gaze flitted until it landed on the family photo on his desk. It was the last one he and Ella had made with the boys before she lost her hair.

This was his chance to tell her about his late wife, but a lump formed in his throat when Dixie's eyes welled with tears.

"You have a beautiful family." She dipped her head to wipe her eyes. "Why me?"

He took a sip of sweet tea to wash down the emotion of the moment, then refocused on the business at hand. "I've been asking myself that very question for over a month. All I do know is that when I think about you heading up this division, it feels right. Nothing else has panned out."

"Tell me about your vision." She leaned back in her chair, leaving her food untouched.

He told her about the need for home health care for those who wanted to receive care or to die at home. He kept it professional, not mentioning his wife for fear of losing his composure. When he finished, her brows were furrowed.

"What is it, Dixie?" He hadn't realized he'd reached out to her until his hand rested on the desk between them.

"Did you know I work in the ICU?"

"I did know. That's one reason why I thought you'd be perfect. You see people on their way out. If there's a way we can help them do it at home, shouldn't we give them the opportunity?"

She nodded, fixing her gaze on a spot on the wall above his head, her mind seemingly faraway. "I think they'd like that very much."

She brought her attention back to him then studied the photo on his desk. "I would love to help you, but I don't think I can."

***

Dixie stood and headed for the door. Before she reached it, it slammed shut in front of her.

A stunning, dark-haired woman stood on the other side of the glass. The expression she wore was similar to one Dixie's mother had used when she'd expected cooperation.

"Do as you know you ought to do." Mama's voice came through loud and clear.

The sudden chill made Dixie hug herself and take a step back. She bumped into Dan.

His hands gripped her upper arms. "Sit down, darlin'. You look like you saw a ghost."

Clenching her fists, she squeezed her eyes shut because the shakes were threatening to seize every muscle in her body. She almost opened her mouth to admit she *had* seen a ghost, but she'd learned early in life people didn't like hearing it, even if it was their loved one she'd seen.

"I'm fine. I apologize. Must be the lack of sleep. I think we should try working together, but I'm not sure you can afford me."

The number he threw out almost made her fall out of the chair she'd just reclaimed. It was more than her other two jobs combined.

"I need you to understand this'll be a lot of work," he said. "You'll be well compensated and have benefits for you and your girls. You'll be calling and visiting a lot of doctors. Maybe even some Congressmen. I might bring your sister in to help with the legal bits, so we can cover our behinds. We're forging new territory here. Are you with me?"

She'd forged some new territory the night she'd met him. Why couldn't she get it out of her head?

She pressed her fingertips to her temples. "I…" She was about to say she'd let him know, but she already knew her answer. If she delayed, she'd most likely see a lot more of the late Mrs. Baker.

"I'm in. My brother has someone to cover my day job after this week. I'll need to give the hospital two weeks' notice. Dan…I mean…" She sighed. "What do you want me to call you?"

"Dan is fine, darlin'. Oh, sorry, not darlin'. I meant, hell, I don't know what to call you either."

She laughed. "D or Dixie is fine. Thank you for this opportunity. I promise to do a good job for you."

"I know you will, darlin'. Dammit." He shook his fist. "I mean, D."

She told him she'd see him in a week then

walked out to her car. With a long exhale, she sagged down in the driver's seat and closed her eyes for a minute.

A knock startled her awake.

She blinked several times, trying to clear her head.

Dan Baker was standing next to her car with a Styrofoam cup in one hand and a to-go plate in the other. "You need a ride?"

She rolled down the window then tucked her hair behind her ears. "No. I'm good."

"Darlin', you've been asleep out here for three hours." He handed her the cup. "Take this coffee. It's black."

"Thank you." She blinked again and sipped the hot liquid. How had she slept in a parking lot for three hours? "I'm good now."

"I read somewhere that driving while sleepy gives you similar reaction times as a drunk driver."

That thought sobered her up quick. She didn't want to be anything like her deceased, drunk-driving husband.

Speaking of dearly departed spouses... "When did your wife pass?"

He lifted his chin and peered down at her. "How do you know she's gone?"

She couldn't tell him the truth, so she shrugged. "I found out very recently."

"So, the misunderstanding is cleared up? You no longer think I'm the kind of man who would cheat on his wife?" His gaze bore into her.

"I'm sorry." She rested her head on the steering wheel and closed her eyes.

It was a long blink, and the next thing she knew Dan was opening her car door.

"You can't drive like this. You'll hurt yourself or someone else. Scoot over. I'll take you wherever you need to go."

"But." She swallowed, chasing the argument as it ran through her brain. "How will you get back?"

"I'll call someone to come pick me up once we get there. Where to, Miss?"

Dixie wanted a sound reason to resist, but she wanted to sleep more. "Home, James."

***

Dan started to tease Dixie about taking her to his home, but she was out of it and probably wouldn't get the joke.

He managed to get her address in Bull Creek before her head lolled to one side and rested on the passenger window.

During the twenty minute drive, he thought about home and what it meant to him now that Ella was gone. It was still home, but he missed having a partner to share it with. He was glad their boys were growing up at Southland. They had plenty of space to roam and a nice house but no mother to tuck them in and kiss their boo-boos.

Once in Bull Creek, he didn't have any trouble finding Church Street. He pulled into the carport, cut the engine, and gently shook Dixie's shoulder. "We're here, darlin'."

He walked around and helped her out of the car.

The carport door to the house opened, and her oldest daughter came out.

"Mama?" The girl looked concerned. "What's wrong?"

"She's fine, honey. Just needs some sleep's all. I'm Dan Baker. You must be Liz."

"Lizabelle." Dixie slurred the name.

"Come on, Mama." Liz put an arm around her mother. "Let's get you to bed. Thank you, Mr. Baker."

He didn't let go of his hold on Dixie. "I need to borrow your phone to call someone to pick me up."

"Good luck getting Katie off of it. She's been on there all afternoon talking to her boyfriend."

Just inside the door was a utility room with a washer and dryer.

"She's a little young for a boyfriend, isn't she?" He turned, edging sideways through the tight space, and had to let go of Dixie, so they could get through the doorway to the kitchen.

"Yes. They call it *going together*." Dixie shook her head. "Thanks again, Dan. Goodnight."

She disappeared down the hallway with Liz, leaving him standing alone on the worn yellow linoleum.

The back door opened, and the little one ran in. She stopped short when she saw him.

The way she took him in made him chuckle.

She started at his boots. Then her gaze moved up and up until her big eyes stared at his face.

He pointed to the stuffed animal she hugged in her arms. "That's a nice horse. He got a name?"

She nodded, eyes wide. "Horsey."

"Looks like someone gave Horsey a haircut." The mane was long in some places and short in others.

"Katie did it. Sometimes, I call him Spike 'cause it feels spikey." She touched the short synthetic fibers with her fingertips.

"Can I see?" Squatting, he held out his hand.

When she gave him the ragged looking horse, he saw someone had also colored Horsey with a magic marker. "It does feel spikey. I'm Dan, by the way."

"What are you doing here?"

"Your mama's going to start working for me, and she was too sleepy to drive, so I brought her home." He returned the stuffed animal. "What's your name?"

"Maddie. You wanna come jump on the trampoline with me?"

He snickered then stood. "I need to use the phone first. Then I'll watch you jump, but I'm afraid I'm so big I might tear it up."

"Oh, okay." Maddie dragged a wooden barstool over to where the phone hung on the wall and climbed up until she stood in the seat.

Dan moved closer to catch her in case she fell. His boys did things like this all the time, but seeing this tiny girl do it made him nervous.

She picked up the receiver and held it to her ear.

From somewhere in the back of the house, Katie yelled, "Hang up the phone."

Maddie calmly spoke, "Excuse me, Katie, but we have company, and he needs to use the phone. Also, stop yelling. Mama's asleep." For the last part, she yelled herself.

It was a wonder Dixie ever slept at all. Dan's chest tightened.

Maddie hung up and counted to ten out loud before she picked up the phone again. She listened for a second then smiled and held it out to him.

"Thank you, sugar."

He called the office and asked for Charlie who, along with his wife, worked for Dan and lived in Bull Creek. After explaining his predicament and telling Charlie where he could find a spare key to the Blazer, Dan hung up.

Three young girls stood in the middle of the kitchen watching him.

"Hey, Mr. Baker," Katie said. "Is our mama really going to work for you?"

"Yes, she is."

"But she already has two jobs," Maddie whined.

"She's going to quit both of those jobs and just have one," he explained. "She'll be home at night, starting in a couple of weeks."

"Mama said you weren't the kind of man she wanted to work for." Liz narrowed her eyes.

"That's because we had a misunderstanding, but it's cleared up now."

"What kind of misunderstanding?" Liz raised her chin.

"Your mama questioned my character because she thought I'd cheated at something. You're very mature, Liz. How old are you?"

"She's only twelve, but everybody who calls here thinks she's a grown-up," Katie said.

"That's true. I thought she was a grown-up

when I called," he said.

"Really?" Liz asked, a big grin on her pretty face.

"Lizabelle, don't grow up too fast. Mama always says that," Maddie said.

"How'd you get the name Lizabelle?"

Katie swung her arms side to side as if she were about to spin in a circle. "Most people call her Liz, but mama used to say Elizabeth, and when Maddie tried to say it, it came out Lizabelle." She spun on one foot.

Dan smiled. He'd been around these girls for less than ten minutes, and they already had him wrapped around their little fingers.

"Are you ladies hungry?" he asked.

"I'm gonna make supper." Liz gestured to the counter where a box of generic macaroni and cheese sat next to a can of tuna.

Dan couldn't stand the thought of them eating that, not while he could do something about it, but their options were limited.

"How 'bout McDonald's?" he asked. "My truck will be here soon, and I can run get the food, or we can all go and eat there, so your mama can rest."

The younger girls looked to Liz. Their bouncing in place and clapping their hands together in a pleading gesture let him know they wanted to go. He, too, looked to Liz since she was clearly the authority when their mama was unavailable.

"I guess it would be okay," Liz said. "Do you think our mama will get mad?" She directed her question to him.

"No. I think she'd be okay with you girls having a treat." He nearly crossed his fingers behind his back.

"I'll go get some money," Liz said.

"It's on me, honey," he said. "Now that your mama will be working for me, it's my pleasure to do this for her and you."

"Good," Katie said. "Because I'm saving my allowance for a new dress."

"I'm saving mine for a horse," Maddie said.

"And what are you saving your money for, Liz?" he asked.

She shrugged. "To help Mama if she needs it."

"There must be something you would buy if you could," he said.

"She wants another book about guitars," Katie said. "She's been practicing from one of our daddy's old books, but some of the pages are stuck together."

"Our daddy rode a bull to heaven," Maddie said.

Dan figured his eyebrows were kissing his hairline. "Was he in a rodeo?"

Liz placed a hand on Maddie's shoulder and shook her head. "Our dad was killed in a car accident in which he hit a bull. The bull also perished." In a loud whisper, she added, "She gets confused."

Dan's gut clenched, and he wanted to wrap his arms around all of these sweet girls.

So he did.

Chapter Seven

The alarm clock woke Dixie. She still felt groggy but jumped up when she saw the time. She needed to be at work in an hour, but it was past her girls' bedtime, and she always tucked them in.

She opened the door to Katie and Maddie's room and found them both sleeping. She kissed each of them before she went to check on Liz.

Before Steve died, the girls had all shared a room. It was a three-bedroom house, but since Dixie and Steve had had separate bedrooms, that had left just one for the girls. They'd believed it was because Dixie worked nights. She hadn't had the heart to tell them their parents' marriage was loveless, and the girls were the only thing keeping them together.

Liz had moved into Steve's room after he died, and that's where Dixie found her sitting in bed, reading.

"Hey, baby. Why'd you reset my alarm?"

She dog-eared the page and closed the book. "You needed the sleep. I put the girls to bed. I know you like to do it, but—"

"It's okay, Lizabelle. I did need the sleep. Thank you for being my big helper." Dixie sat on the side of the bed and brushed Liz's hair away from her face.

Liz leaned into her hand. "I'm glad you're going to work for Mr. Baker. He's very nice."

"Yeah? I think this could be very good for us. I'll be making more money and can make my own hours."

"We got you some dinner. I put it in the oven on warm."

Dixie pursed her lips. "I thought you were making tuna casserole."

"Mr. Baker treated us to McDonald's. We got you a fish fillet with no sauce, like you like." Liz's big blue eyes were hopeful.

"So, Mr. Baker bought your affection with a Big Mac and the girls' with Happy Meals?" The corner of her mouth twitched.

"You're not mad, are you?"

"No, honey. I'm not mad." She patted Liz's hand and squeezed. "You girls need to write him a thank you note, and I'll put it in the mail."

"I'm here," Miss Spann called from the living room.

"I better go say hello and get ready for work. G'night, honey." Dixie kissed the top of Liz's head.

Her retired neighbors, Miss Spann and Mrs. Whitmore, took turns spending the night at her house with the girls. They were sisters who'd moved in together after Mr. Whitmore passed. They'd offered to help after Steve died, so between Dixie's niece, Sheila, and *the old gals* as Liz jokingly called them behind their backs, Dixie's girls were covered.

Dixie told Miss Spann about her new job, and the chattier of the two sisters had a lot of questions. Not surprisingly, most of them were about the handsome young man who'd taken the girls out for dinner.

She had lots of advice when she learned he was Dixie's new employer. Being that Miss Spann was pushing seventy and had never married, Dixie was disinclined to take her guidance to heart.

When Dixie walked out of the hospital the next morning, she found Dan Baker leaning against the side of her car with a large Styrofoam cup in each hand.

"Hey," she said. "I just gave my notice. So in two weeks, I'm all yours."

A naughty smirk landed on his lips, and she regretted how she'd phrased her comment even as liquid heat rushed through her veins.

He handed her one of the cups. "That's the best news I've heard all day."

"Um, it's only seven fifteen in the morning." She inhaled the rich, black coffee aroma before she sipped it.

"Even so," he said.

"Thanks for feeding my girls and me last night." The smile she offered was genuine.

"They're precious. I'm impressed with how well-mannered they are. I hope people say the same about my boys when I'm not around." His deep voice sent a shiver across her skin.

"Thank you. I hate to cut this short, but I have to boogie. Gotta get the girls on the bus and get ready for round two."

"Actually, that's why I'm here. I spoke to your brother last night, and he's got you covered. As of today, you start working for me. I don't expect eight hours or anything, not for two weeks when you're done with your nights here."

He reached behind him and picked up several file folders from the hood of her car. "This is the employment contract, tax forms, the start of the business plan, you know, the boring stuff. Don't come into the office yet. You can do this from home. Start working on it a-little-along, and call me with an update later."

She opened the top folder and picked up a check made out to her. Her pulse raced faster. "What's this?"

"Hiring bonus. It should help ease the transition until your first real paycheck." He winked.

"I can't accept this. I haven't earned it yet." She tried to give it to him and at the same time force backseat memories from her head.

"Believe me, you will." He pushed her hand away, his touch scorching her. "For those weeks when you put in fifty or sixty hours, you will have earned it then."

"Dan, I don't know what to say." An errant tear snuck down her cheek, and she swiped at it.

"You don't have to say anything, darlin'." He

reached out and stopped another tear with his thumb. "Go get those sweet girls ready for school."

After she put the girls on the bus, Dixie sat at the dining table and stared at the check. It was almost enough to pay off Steve's debt with the bookie. A huge burden would be lifted when it was done.

On the other hand, the girls needed dance recital costumes, and Katie's birthday was coming up soon. All she'd asked for was to be in the Little Miss Bull Creek pageant.

Dixie stuck the check in her purse. She'd decide what to do with it after she deposited it.

Looking over the forms, she filled in the necessary information. Dan Baker was a generous employer. The medical plan was better than what she had with the hospital, and that was a great plan. For the retirement plan, he matched up to ten percent of her contributions. The hospital only matched four percent.

She felt like she'd won a prize and got a little nervous that someone might try to snatch it away from her. Someone always did.

Dixie rubbed her tired eyes and shuffled to her room to get some rest.

When she'd been lying down for few minutes, the bed jostled as someone lay down beside her.

Opening her eyes, she turned to see nothing.
No one was there.

Chapter Eight

Sitting at his desk, Dan hugged the three handwritten thank you notes to his chest. Maddie had drawn a horse while Katie had drawn a little yellow-haired girl in a pink dress. Liz hadn't drawn anything, but she did put a heart over the *i* in her name.

Smiling, he tucked the papers in his top desk drawer. If he ever needed a pick-me-up, these would do the trick. They really were sweet girls, and he adored them.

He checked his watch then rushed out the door. He'd missed the last two weeks of Boy Scouts, and since he was an assistant Scoutmaster, he really needed to show up this time.

He'd forgotten about Reba until the end of scouts when she came to pick up her son, which her ex-husband normally did.

She circled Dan like a vulture then pounced, gripping his arm with her manicured nails. "Thanks for inviting Billy to Johnny's birthday party this Saturday. I'll be bringing him."

She winked and gave a seductive smile. "I'll be glad to stay after and help you clean up."

"Much appreciated, but Aunt May doesn't like anyone interfering in her process. She'll have it under control." He attempted but failed to move out of her grasp.

"I still want to make dinner for you sometime, handsome. Maybe we can talk on Saturday and set something up." She poked him in the chest with her finger.

Before he could tell her he wasn't interested because he wasn't over Ella, their boys interrupted.

She gave him another wink and a finger wave as she walked away with extra sway in her generous hips.

When he got his boys home and settled, he dialed Dixie's number.

"Lizabelle." He grinned when he recognized her polite, mature phone voice. "It's Dan Baker."

"Hello," she said. "Mama's putting the girls to bed, but she should be available to speak to you momentarily."

"Where in the world did you learn such a big word?" He leaned back in the office chair in his bedroom.

"I read a lot. I try to use proper grammar on the telephone. Living here in the South, we get it wrong in everyday conversation most of the time." Her clear tone held a touch of warmth.

He chuckled. "I'm the worst of all, honey. Do you know if y'all have plans for Saturday?"

"Not that I'm aware of."

"My son, Johnny, is having his eleventh birthday party, and I'd like you girls to come. There'll be go-carts."

The gasp he heard over the phone line made him belly laugh. "I guess girls like go-carts, too."

"Yes, sir. Oh, here's Mama. Hold please."

There was excited jabbering before Dixie picked up. "If you wanted to tempt Lizabelle, you couldn't have made a better offer."

The tension in his shoulders fell away like autumn leaves. "It was a long shot. I have no idea what girls like."

"She likes to drive. Her dad used to take her out on the back roads and let her practice."

"She'll have plenty of pig trails to ride out here at Southland."

"What's Johnny into?" she asked. "I know nothing about little boys."

"He's getting into comic books. I have, make that *had*, a small assortment. He discovered them and has been hooked. Now he saves his allowance, so he can add to the collection."

"We'll see what we can come up with. I have one question though. Will my girls be the only females at the party?"

"Don't worry. I won't let anything happen to them. A few of Johnny's friends have sisters who were also invited."

He paused and cleared his throat. "Oh, and one more thing. When you come, bring the business plan, and we'll sit down for a few minutes after the party to brainstorm."

When he hung up, Dan smiled to himself.

Everything in his master plan was coming together, but she'd never be the wiser.

***

Dixie slowed to take the turn into the driveway at Dan's place.

Dense pines lined the road, but balloons were attached to the white wooden fence on either side of the entrance to mark the spot for the celebration. A small carved wooden sign read *SOUTHLAND*.

Nostalgia swept over Dixie at the sight, reminding her of home so much she could almost hear her daddy's voice. Her family's estate had been called Sutherland, after the first Triple Crown winner her daddy had trained.

"What kind of place is this, Mama?" Maddie asked.

"This is where Mr. Dan lives with his sons." Dixie swallowed, nervous at the idea of meeting his children.

"What are their names again?" Katie asked.

"Danny, Johnny, and Paul," Dixie said.

"They're only missing George and Ringo." Liz laughed.

Dixie shot her eldest a sideways glance. "They might not appreciate your humor, honey."

"I bet Mr. Baker would get it," she said.

"Horses! Mama, look! There're horses." Maddie bounced up and down in the backseat.

"I see them, baby. Take it easy, and do not ask to ride or pet them. This is a go-cart party, and I bet the horses are out here, so the noise won't scare them."

"But, Mama—"

"Madelyn Nicole Johnson, don't make me turn this car around." Dixie broke out her mom voice.

"Okay, Mama. I'll…be…good." All spoken between sobs while alligator tears rolled down her cheeks.

If Dixie were a surfer, she could ride the wave of guilt swamping her.

"Shh. It's okay, Maddie," Katie soothed. "We get to ride on go-carts, and that'll be fun. You'll see."

Dixie glanced in the rearview mirror and blinked to clear her vision. "Katie, are you wearing lipstick?"

"Duh." Nothing but attitude coming from her pageant princess. "You wouldn't let me wear a dress, so I had to do something to make me look like a girl." She tossed her hair over her shoulder.

Dixie gritted her teeth and prepared to tongue lash her precious child until she was distracted by a man directing traffic. She slowed and rolled down the window.

"You Miss Dixie?" the traffic man asked.

"I am." She nodded once.

"I figured when I see all dem purty girls piled in there. We need to park your car 'round da other side since you're staying after the party. I'se be happy to do it faw ya."

"Sure." She paused. "What's your name, sir?"

"Big Dan and the boys call me Uncle Ben Hill. Course, we ain't related by blood, but we family all the same."

That was obvious since his skin was the color

of baking chocolate. A flash of childhood adoration rose in her chest at the memory of her Granny Bite. Until she'd passed, her nanny, Tobitha, had been Dixie's favorite person other than her daddy. But then, Granny never really left, not for many years.

"I know how that goes." Dixie hoped to convey all she felt in those simple words. "Thank you, Mr. Ben Hill. I need one minute." She held up her finger and turned in her seat.

"Katherine Marie Johnson. If you ever say *duh* to me again, I will knock you into next week. Madelyn Nicole, no horses. Leave Spike the Horsey in the car. Elizabeth Ann—"

"What did I do?" Liz's eyes were wide and wary.

Dixie pointed. "Watch the joking. They don't know your sense of humor."

Liz saluted her. "Yes, ma'am, Dixie Jensen Johnson. Now that we've all heard our full names, can we get to the party?"

"You're not too big for me to switch, young lady." She inhaled deeply. "Don't embarrass me, girls. Please. This is my boss. We have to look like we have it together, even if we don't."

"But that's lying," Maddie said.

"It's being fake," Liz said.

"We can do this, sisters." Katie flipped her hair over her shoulder again. "Who says we don't have it together? Put your smiles on and let's go."

Dixie couldn't have been prouder.

"Advice from the beauty queen," Liz mumbled as she climbed out of the car.

Standing still, as Mr. Ben Hill drove her car

away, Dixie took a moment to admire the large, rustic home of wood and stone. It was very manly, very Dan-ly. She bit back her smile.

Ben Hill had told them to go around the side of the house to the back.

Once Dixie spied fifty kids and almost as many adults scattered among them, she nearly ran back for the car. In the middle of it all, she spotted Dan amid a gaggle of women. Fierce and unfounded envy danced into her heart, clouding all rational thought.

Her lips twisted and she narrowed her eyes. His bereavement was clearly at an end.

***

When Dan spotted Dixie and her girls walking toward the table, which held a ridiculous amount of presents for Johnny, his heart lifted. He extracted himself from the claws of the divorcees who'd treed him like a pack of coon dogs on the scent.

"Hi, Mr. Baker," Liz said.

"Hey, ladies. I'm glad you're here. Come on. I want to introduce you to my boys."

He found them in the line of kids who were waiting their turn for the go-carts. Fifteen two-seater go-carts still left a dozen kids standing around. His boys were graciously letting the others ride because they'd been riding all morning before the party started.

He introduced Danny, who was thirteen and a half, Johnny the eleven-year-old birthday boy, and Paul, his eight-year-old. He also introduced Danny's best bud, Jason.

"Danny, why don't you and Jason take the

younger girls for rides first? Liz, I think you can manage, but let Johnny ride with you to show you the course," Dan instructed.

"This is quite a set up you have here," Dixie said, a hint of admiration in her tone.

"The boys and I made the course this morning. Good times. Would you like to go for a ride?" Dan asked, wriggling his eyebrows.

"Maybe later. The kids won't like it if the grown-ups steal their turns."

"I could actually use your help after the guests go. We'll have to drive all the go-carts back out to the road, so my buddy Jack can load them up on his transport vehicle."

She nodded. "What does Jack do with so many go-carts?"

"He owns several cart tracks and miniature golf courses in and around Atlanta. He closed one of the tracks today, so we could use the carts."

"He must be a good friend." She looked dubious.

"He ain't doing it for free, darlin'. Man's gotta make a livin'."

"It's good you're in a position to do this for your son. They're handsome boys and polite to boot." She nodded in their direction.

A bubble of pride swelled in him. "Thank you. They get their looks from me and their manners from their mother."

"A good combination." A dazzling smile alighted on her lips.

Dan didn't notice anyone else for a long moment. But as he escorted her to the food table, he saw the looks they were getting, and his hackles rose. "I better introduce you around."

Later, when they were wrangling up the kids for lunch and birthday cake, Danny parked a go-cart close to the crowd and leapt from the vehicle. "Dad, Paul got hurt."

Paul got out of the cart, cradling his hand, tear tracks staining his cheeks.

"What happened?" Dan dropped to his knees in front of his youngest son.

"His hand was outside the cart, and we skidded into a tree. He hit it pretty hard."

The knuckles and back of Paul's right hand were skinned and bloody.

Dan scooped him up and headed inside, where there was a first aid kit.

"Can I help?" Dixie asked from behind him.

A rush of air escaped Dan's lungs. "Please." He moved to the side a little. "Paul, Miss Dixie's a nurse, and she's gonna take a look at it and fix you up. Okay, son?"

"'Kay, Daddy." Paul sniffed.

Dan walked toward the kitchen. "Where do you want him, D?"

"Set him on the table."

Aunt May placed the first aid kit within reach and stood back while Dixie looked inside and pulled out gauze and a bottle of mercurochrome.

"Can I get a bowl of water, please?"

Dan moved to get it, but Aunt May shooed him away.

"Okay, cute stuff. We need to put your hand in the water to rinse off the dirt and tree bark. It might hurt a little, but I think you're very tough and brave. Am I right?"

Paul nodded.

"Okay, wiggle your toes."

When he did, she dipped his hand into the water and used some gauze to rub the wound. "Keep going. Don't stop."

Dan had heard those words from her before but in an entirely different context. His face flamed.

When Dixie pulled Paul's hand out of the water, Aunt May handed her a clean towel.

"Thank you." She smiled. "Paul, you're tougher than I thought. Hold your hand up. I need to check the bones and make sure nothing's broken."

She used her fingertips to gently assess his hand. "That looks good. Now for the hard part."

She held up the mercurochrome bottle. "This stuff burns, but it kills the germs, so you won't get an infection."

"I hate it." Paul's shoulders shook as he cried harder.

"Shh, honey. It's okay." Dixie rubbed Paul's back. "I know a few tricks that'll help. Can I tell you?"

He nodded, and she wiped his face with the towel.

"Okay, left arm up. Flex your muscle." She squeezed his biceps. "Very nice. You're gonna have muscles as big as your dad's someday. Let it go."

Dan watched her work her calming magic on Paul, and he himself was more relaxed. They took deep breaths together and let them out slowly.

"Okay, next time we hold our breath, I'll put

the medicine on. Then we'll blow on your hand, so it won't feel so bad. Ready?"

"Wait," Paul said. "Daddy, will you help us blow?"

"You bet I will, buddy."

"Smart thinking, cutie." Dixie tweaked Paul's nose and winked.

Dan's heart felt like it had crashed into a tree, and this woman held it in her healing hands.

"Here we go. Show me your muscle again." Dixie took a big breath and held it while she applied the medicine.

When it was over, Paul said he barely felt it at all. Dixie bandaged his hand with the gauze and secured it with medical tape.

Dan wrapped both arms around Dixie. "Thank you, darlin'. It sure is nice having you around."

Chapter Nine

Dixie reveled in Dan's appreciation, and she savored his strong embrace.

Aunt May shot her a wide-eyed look, so Dixie quickly disentangled herself from him.

Dan lifted Paul into his arms. "Let's go get something to eat."

Dixie started cleaning up the aftermath. "Thank you for your help, Miss May."

"You welcome, honey. Be careful. Dem other ladies gone try to get rid o' ya."

Dixie frowned. "What ladies?" When she turned toward the windows across the back of the house, the hens scattered.

"Oh." Maybe she wasn't the only one with a jealous streak when it came to Big Dan Baker.

While she gathered her courage to return to the party, she finished helping May clean up the mess she'd made on the dining table.

Before stepping back outside, Dixie took a

moment to peruse the interior.

The house was homey. The heaviness of the wood walls and floors was offset by light drapes and decorative accents, revealing a feminine touch. There were several family pictures in the den.

Seeing them made her sad because her last family picture with Steve and the girls had been taken when Maddie was a baby.

Leaving the cozy den, she walked out to the back porch and saw Liz and Katie at a table eating burgers with some new friends.

She searched the crowd for Maddie but didn't see her. "Girls, where's your sister?"

They both looked around, and Liz stood.

"What's wrong, darlin'?" Dan asked Dixie.

"Have you seen Maddie?" Her anxiety made her words come out high and strained.

"Don't panic. She couldn't have gone far," he said.

Liz grimaced. "Mama, she might have gone to see the horses."

"She's small enough to squeeze between the fence boards," Dan said. "Let's ride out there and see."

He led Dixie into the barn, where he climbed onto a four-wheeler and cranked it up. "Hop on."

Without thinking, she climbed on and wrapped her arms around his waist. When she realized her error, she loosened her grip. He would be easy to cling to, especially while she was worried about Maddie.

He drove out into the pasture toward the road. When she spotted Maddie among the horses, Dixie let out a sigh of relief and hugged Dan from behind.

Still a little ways off, he stopped the four-wheeler and cut the engine, twisting his head and shoulders to make eye contact. "I know you're upset but take it easy on her. She loves horses, and it was too much to ask her to stay away from 'em."

Dixie knew he was right, but her relief at seeing Maddie unhurt turned to anger that she'd disobeyed.

As Dixie approached her daughter, Maddie looked up with frightened eyes.

"I'm sorry, Mama." Her lip quivered as tears fell. All the while, one of her small hands rested on a horse's side.

The anger melted as Dixie's heart warmed at seeing her baby with her first love. Horses had been Dixie's first love, too.

She dropped to her knees. "Come here, baby. Do you know why I'm upset?"

"'Cause you said no horses."

"I'm only a tiny bit upset about that. I'm more upset because you disappeared, and I didn't know where you were. I thought you might be hurt, and it scared me."

"I'm sorry, Mama. I didn't mean to scare you." Her voice dropped to a whisper. "The lady was with me."

Dixie looked around but didn't see the lady Maddie spoke of.

"Am I gonna get a spanking?"

Dan snickered, and Dixie cut her eyes at him. She had to press her lips together tightly to keep from smiling.

"I don't think this deserves a spanking, but it does deserve some punishment. I'll think about it and let you know."

"I have a question," Dan said. "How do you like the horses, sugar?"

"I love them. They're beautiful, and I think this one likes me." She petted the horse's shoulder.

"Yeah, that's Ringo. He likes all the pretty girls."

Dixie smiled at the name, knowing Liz would get a huge kick out of it.

"We better get back and have some birthday cake," Dan said. "If your mom says it's okay, I'll let you see them again later. But remember, you can't go by yourself. That's the rule."

"Oh, Dan." Dixie squeezed her temples. "I'm so sorry about keeping you from Johnny's party. Next time, you'll think twice before inviting the Johnson women over."

"Don't worry your pretty little head, darlin'. The Johnson women are welcome anytime. You fixed my boy up. The least I could do was help you find little sugarfoot here."

Dan put Maddie in front of him on the ATV, and Dixie, once again, sat behind him. She was grateful for Dan and his kindness. If she let him, he would sneak into her heart, and she couldn't afford to have that happen.

When they were back in the barn, Maddie bowed her head and kicked at the dirt. "Mr. Baker, I'm sorry I broke the rules and made you miss the party. Please don't fire my mama."

"I won't fire your mama, sugar. I need her too

much. You just don't forget that the rules are there to protect you, okay?"

"Okay." Maddie wrapped her arms around Dan's legs.

"Come here, sugar, and let me hold you a second." He picked her up and hugged her to his chest.

A rush of warmth overtook Dixie at seeing her daughter handled so lovingly. It was followed by a longing to be held that way herself.

***

Dan stood as near as possible to watch Johnny open his gifts while a mass of kids crowded around.

His son got everything from Frisbees, Nerf footballs, and other various sporting equipment to board games, books, and no less than four Rubik's Cubes.

Liz had volunteered to sit next to Johnny and make a list of the gift and the giver, so he could write thank you cards later.

As she passed him the last present, she said, "This is from us. It has sentimental value."

Johnny tore the paper and opened the lid of the box. "Dad. Golly, Dad. Look. We don't have these." He held up a stack of comic books.

Dan's jaw went slack. *Where had they found such a rare treat?*

They were the first ten issues of the Fantastic Four from the early sixties.

"This is so cool. Thanks." Johnny half-hugged Liz.

"I hope it's okay that they aren't brand new, but they were our dad's," Liz said. "Mama told us you like comics, and we decided to give you these for your collection."

"That's very sweet, honey," Dan said then glanced around for Dixie.

She was on the porch swing, looking right at home with Maddie stretched out, sleeping with her head on Dixie's lap.

He walked over and leaned against the rail. "Johnny loves the gift. Are you sure the girls are okay with giving them up?"

"It was their idea. They wanted someone to have them who'd appreciate them."

"Ella always gave the boys sentimental gifts instead of new toys. I really appreciate it, darlin'."

"Do you call all of your employees *darlin'*, Big Dan?" Reba's shrill voice grated on his last nerve. Or maybe it was her tone.

He rolled his eyes before he pasted a smile on his face and turned to her. "Reba, I've been looking all over for you."

"You have?" She fanned herself with a paper plate .

"I thought you wanted to talk about dinner. Let's go for a walk." Dan took her arm and led her away from the crowd.

"I'm so glad you're wanting to come over."

"Actually, Reba, I don't think I can yet. I still see Ella every time I turn around. I don't know if I'll ever get over losing her."

"Bless your heart, you poor thing." She patted his chest. "You take your time, Big Dan. And call me when you're ready."

He didn't like the way she said his name, with

the emphasis on *Big*, as if she knew something intimate about him. Besides his late wife, there'd only been one other woman. If he had his way, Dixie Johnson would remain that exclusive one.

He shouldn't be thinking it, but he was. Dixie had gotten into his head the night she'd gotten into his Blazer, and he hadn't been able to forget her. He'd sensed there was something pure and sweet about the woman despite what they'd done.

She hadn't pretended like she did hit and runs every day. She'd been nervous and a little clumsy. Out of practice, just like him. It had still been sexy, and if he thought about it too much, he'd get turned on all over again.

He needed to concentrate on letting Reba down gently and to get her to stop rubbing his arm. He supposed she was trying to be comforting, but it was annoying the hell out of him.

"I really appreciate your invitation, but I can't accept it. Not yet."

"I understand, and I want you to know I'm always here if you need to talk."

"You are too kind, Reba. Thank you for bringing Billy. He and Johnny always have fun together. And thanks for the Rubik's Cube."

As he watched her walk away, he realized Dixie was the only person who'd asked what Johnny would like. And her gift had been the best of them all.

He'd promised to be professional when he hired Dixie, but his heart wasn't going along with that plan. It had a mind of its own, and it was falling fast.

Chapter Ten

Dixie cackled louder than she had in a long time.

As she raced Dan to the end of the driveway, she pressed the pedal of the go-cart down as far as it would go. They were probably going all of ten miles an hour since Jack had put something on the engines to keep the kids from going too fast.

As a mom, Dixie was glad to know it. But the wind in her hair gave her a thrill not unlike the one she'd had as a child when she'd raced and jumped show horses. She wanted just a little bit more.

After she parked and got off, she still vibrated with the thrill of the ride.

As they walked back to the house, Dan bumped his arm into her shoulder. "You wouldn't have won if I didn't have a hundred pounds on you."

"A hundred pounds? No way. I look lighter than I am." She regretted it as soon as it left her mouth. It might sound like she was fishing for a compliment.

"You look fantastic no matter what the scale says, darlin'."

"Thanks, but I think we should curtail the flirting. We work together, remember?"

"Of course, I remember. I hope the pet names don't offend you, but once I call someone a nickname a few times, it gets stuck in my thick head, and it's hard to change."

"I love the pet names you have for my girls, but you should be more careful around me. Reba Red-claws won't be the only person to notice if you keep calling me darlin'."

"I know you're right. I'm sorry, dah...I mean D."

He smirked. "That sounded like an Indian name you invented for Reba. We have a little Cherokee in the lineage. My grandpa used to tell me all these proverbs, but I think he borrowed many of them or just plain made them up."

Dixie smiled, remembering the toast Dan had made the night they met—*all dreams spin out from the same web*. Her father had said it many times. She was pretty certain it was Hopi.

"My grandpa also made up Indian names for people," Dan said. "What would you call me?"

"Huh?" She forced herself back into the present.

"My Indian name?"

In the twilight, she could make out his white teeth, which were the first thing about him that had attracted her.

Think, D. Man. Indian heritage. Name. "I can

tell, now that you mention it. The cheekbones. Very—" She stopped the word sexy from coming out of her mouth just in time. "High."

"Uh-huh." He was smirking again, like he was on to her.

Focus, Dixie. Handsome Dan. No! Buffalo Dan. No!

What was big and strong yet kind and gentle? *Dan Baker.*

"I don't know." She flipped her palms up. "Clydesdale Dan."

"That's almost like saying Big Dan."

"No, it isn't. Not to someone who knows horses. Sure, they're big and so are you, height wise, but they're intelligent, hard-workers who are merciful and yielding—"

"You think I'm intelligent?"

Her steps faltered, his incredulity catching her by surprise. "Of course, I do. I also respect you a great deal. Everyone does."

Dumbfounded was not a look she thought she'd ever see on Dan's face.

The next words left her mouth without hesitation. "How can a plain woman like me astound so great a man?"

Not so gently, he pounced, his lips claiming hers with ferocity. Her mind reeled, her fingers threaded through his dark hair as her mouth opened to let him in.

She didn't know how long they were lip-locked before the sounds of children forced her to pull away.

Dan blinked several times and tried to close the

distance she'd put between them.

She pushed against a wall of muscle. "We have company."

The kiss had been perfect, and she'd wanted it so badly she didn't chastise him or herself for allowing it. But she did try to shake it off and stop panting.

As they continued walking, the kids ran to greet them.

***

Dan held his breath and tried to rein in his thoughts. It was strange having Dixie in his bedroom, even though it doubled as his home office.

As she sat at his desk, all he could think about was carrying her eight feet to the bed and doing some manual labor.

May and Ben Hill were taking down the party decorations with the help of all the kids, except Maddie, because May kept telling her she was too little to help. She also kept giving Maddie slices of leftover cake, which Dixie said might send her into a diabetic coma.

Dan sat beside her in a folding chair while she told him what she'd discovered from talking to her doctor friends.

Hours passed while they worked on the finishing touches of the business plan, but it seemed like no time at all.

"You're a pioneer, Dan. Blazing the way for future generations."

"You have to stop complimenting me, dah…I mean, Dixie. It makes me want to kiss you again."

She blushed and dipped her head, giving him a shy smile. "That isn't my intention."

"I know, dah...hell, Dixie—"

Raised voices made him lose his train of thought.

"Uh-oh." She stood.

"Give it back, you cotton-headed girlie girl." Venom laced Danny's words.

Dan opened the bedroom door in time to see Johnny step in front of Katie and square off against his older, bigger brother.

"Boys." Dan strode into the room. "Daniel Ethan Baker, you better have a damn good reason for raising your voice at a woman."

"She's a little thief. She stole my picture."

"He said mean things." Katie peeked around Johnny.

"Katherine Marie Johnson, what have I told you about tattling?" Dixie asked.

"But, Mama—"

"Sit down on the couch right now before I bend you over my knee." Dixie pointed to the sofa. "Give me that pocket book."

Katie started crying as she handed the little pink purse to her mama. Dan's heart broke for the little girl.

Dixie pulled out a picture and looked at it for a moment before she handed it to Dan.

"I told you she stole it." Danny's chin jutted out over his puffed up chest.

"Boy." Dan's ire rose into his throat, clogging it, so a low growl resounded. "This is my picture. Do you care to tell me how you got it?"

"You didn't even miss it." A whole lot of teenage attitude pulsed from Danny.

"If you like your teeth in your mouth, you better watch your tone, young man." His own teeth ached from his muscles holding them tightly together. "Tell me why you took it?"

"I miss her, okay. I have a picture of her with hair, but this's how she looked in the end. I wanted it." Danny crossed his arms over his chest.

Dan studied the black and white photo he'd hired a photographer to take a few weeks before Ella passed.

He was sitting on their bed, leaning against the headboard, and she was between his legs. His lips were on her bald head while it rested against his chest. Even then, she was stunningly beautiful.

Dixie wiped tears from her eyes. "Katie, why did you take something that doesn't belong to you?"

"Lizabelle found it and asked if the bald lady was his mama—"

"I didn't mean to sound so insensitive," Liz said. "I apologize."

"Then," Katie cried, "he said no one would ever love my mama like his daddy loved his."

"Danny." Dan nearly gasped. "How could you say something like that?"

Danny's eyes were down in contrition, and he shrugged. "I don't want their gold-digging mama to move in with all her brats."

Dan took two steps and grabbed Danny by the arms. "You apologize for that right this second, or I'll take you out to the woodshed and tear your ass out of the frame."

"Dan," Dixie said, "take it easy on him. This may be a misunderstanding, like when we first met. Don't discipline him in anger. Please."

Knowing she spoke sense, he let Danny go and planted his fists on his hips.

"Danny, will you sit down and talk to us a minute?" Dixie asked.

He plopped down but didn't speak until Dan thumped his ear. "Yes, ma'am."

"First," Dixie began, "Katie, you know it's wrong to steal."

"Yes, ma'am."

"Danny got upset and said those things because he misses his mom so much. You know how you miss your daddy sometimes?"

"Yes, ma'am."

"You wouldn't like it if someone came in and took your picture of you and your daddy when you won your pageant, would you?"

"No, ma'am, but I wouldn't say mean things."

"Honey, you might say mean things. Not to be cruel but to retaliate. It's human nature. If someone does something that hurts us, we want to hurt them back."

"That's right, Katie." Dan finally had control of his temper enough to contribute to the parenting.

He sat on the couch next to Katie and rubbed her back. "Part of growing up is learning not to strike out when people do hurtful things. But that doesn't mean you have to be a doormat and let someone take advantage of you or treat you badly either. It's not okay *ever* for a man to yell at a woman in anger." He glared at his oldest son.

"What Mr. Dan's saying is that you have to take the high road. People might not know the things they say are hurting your feelings. You shouldn't assume malice." Dixie's voice was as calm as the eye of a hurricane.

"What's malice, Mama?" Maddie asked.

"It means that someone has evil intentions. They intend to crush your spirit." Liz narrowed her eyes at Danny.

Dan watched Liz who stood near the door with her hands on Maddie's shoulders, looking ready to bolt if things got bad. Liz's intelligence intimidated him a little.

"I don't want to crush anyone's…ah, soul or whatever," Danny said.

"We know, Danny." Dixie turned back to her middle child. "Also, think about what he said, Katie baby, and use logic. How could he possibly know how much anyone will ever love me? Can he see the future?"

"He might be like you, Mama…and Maddie. You see things—" Katie started.

"Um, baby. No." Dixie shook her head.

"Yeah, Mama," Maddie said. "The lady—"

"Madelyn, hush." Dixie gave her youngest a pointed look.

Startled by the seriousness of her tone, Dan wondered what he was missing.

"Sorry." Dixie smiled. "We're getting off topic. Anyway, Danny, I need you to know I'm not what you think I am. I'm willing to work hard to earn my way and take care of my girls. Is that okay with you?"

"Yes, ma'am. I don't really think you're a gold-digger. You're nice, and you took care of Paul. I just saw all those ladies at the party, and Jason said that's what they are. I never heard it before today. I'm sorry for saying it." He never looked her in the eye.

Dan would get him about that later.

"You're forgiven," Dixie said.

Dan couldn't believe his oldest son had just matured before his eyes. Was it Dixie having an adult conversation with him? Or would he have come to the decision on his own?

He marveled at his son until he realized he was thinking about a teenager who made decisions on impulse. But he was still a good boy.

Dixie was the catalyst, so Dan refocused his admiration on the source.

Chapter Eleven

Dixie was mortified at her daughters' behavior. All three of them.

She looked to Dan. "Thank you, and I'm sorry. I'm going to take my girls and go." She gritted her teeth. "Girls, get in the car."

The objections were silenced when she gave them *the look* she'd perfected over the years.

"Dixie, you don't have to go," Dan said.

She smiled a smile she didn't feel. "We can finish up on Monday."

She stood and walked toward the back door. "It was nice to meet you boys. Girls, what do you say?"

"Thank you for inviting us," Liz said.

"We enjoyed it," Katie said.

"Yeah," Maddie said.

"We were glad to have you," Dan said. "Boys."

"Thanks for coming," Danny said.

"Thank you for my gift. It was my favorite." Johnny hugged each of the girls and Dixie.

"Thank you for fixing my hand." Paul embraced Dixie. "Come back anytime." He waved his injured arm at the girls.

"I'll walk you out." Dan put his hand on Dixie's back.

In the driveway, he gave each of the girls a hug before they got in the car.

"I hope they weren't too upset by what happened," he said to Dixie. "I hope you weren't either."

She laughed to keep from crying. It was a miracle he hadn't fired her on the spot. "I'm fine, and they will be when the sting of the switch wears off."

He took her hand and placed her palm on his chest. "Take it easy on 'em, darlin'. They didn't mean any harm, and no one got hurt."

"I'll think about it." She sighed. "Will you do me a favor?"

"Anything."

"Take it easy on the boys and…"

"What?"

"Explain to Danny that it's not like that between us—that I'm not coming on to you. I mean, I know I did that once, but it was before—"

He put a finger over her lips. "I'll take care of it. Don't take what he said to heart. You and I know the truth of it, and we're all that need to know."

She nodded. "Goodnight and thanks again."

"Drive safe, dah-Dixie. That might have to be your new name. I'm having trouble getting it right." His eyes creased at the corners.

With a grin, she got into the car.

"Mama, are we in trouble?" Katie asked.

"You're damn skippy. We're lucky I still have a job."

Liz sighed, and Katie and Maddie cried until they fell asleep.

Dixie used the drive time to think. She hadn't been as upset by the gold-digger remark as she was by what Danny had said about no one ever loving her like Dan had loved Ella.

She'd never be able to get the photograph out of her mind. It was the sweetest and saddest thing she'd ever seen.

Ella had been lucky to have been loved so deeply. Dixie didn't think Steve had ever loved her that much, even in the early years.

She longed to be loved and cherished that way. She wanted the same for her girls. Knowing Dan had the capacity to love so completely made him even more attractive than he already was.

Dixie let out a long breath, needing to put him out of her mind. It was inappropriate to consider a relationship with him. She would focus on the work, not the boss.

There was an opportunity she hadn't talked to Dan about yet. One of her doctor friends, Dr. Flirt was her nickname for him, had told her about a convention in Las Vegas for medical personnel who provided end-stage care for terminal patients.

She hadn't mentioned it because she knew Dan would send her, all expenses paid. Something about that made her feel…indebted. It shouldn't, but it did. It was still a couple of months away, so she would address it later.

She didn't want to leave her girls for the weekend either. Now that she had a normal work schedule, she loved seeing them when she wasn't half asleep.

Dan had been generous about letting her set her hours and work from home because as a single dad, he needed the same flexibility. Of course, he was the boss, so he could make whatever schedule he wanted, and no one could question it.

Dixie felt so blessed for her arrangement that she vowed not to ruin it by having romantic feelings toward her boss or ever allowing her girls around him again.

On one hand, they were precious. On the other, they were sassy and defiant. Her girls, in the wrong mood, might land her in the unemployment line.

No matter how rough the day had been, Dixie wasn't looking forward to the next one. She'd set up a time to meet the bookie, Eddie, at the horse track to pay off the remainder of Steve's debt.

She hated being near the man because of the way he looked at her, like he was imagining her *nekkid*.

Each time they met, she was afraid he would raise the debt or add interest because each time she delivered a payment, he suggested a way she could work it off.

While their next meeting should be their last, she had a bad feeling he would demand something else from her.

***

The next afternoon, Dan was almost to Dixie's house when she pulled her car out of the drive. He

Fool With My Heart

should've called, but he'd wanted to check on her and the girls in person.

Making a snap decision, he followed her. On the off chance she was going to the grocery store, he could still catch her.

The night before, he'd tossed and turned, unable to get her off of his mind. He needed to tread carefully or risk losing her forever, but if he was right, there was something between them—something they needed to explore.

She turned onto the highway to Atlanta, so it appeared she wasn't going to the grocery store after all. He almost turned around, but something urged him on. Probably lust.

He couldn't have been more surprised when, twenty minutes later, she turned into the horse track.

He never figured her for a gambler, but maybe that explained why her kids wore hand-me-down clothes and shoes, which didn't quite fit. He wasn't judging her for it because he'd grown up in want of some things, but if she was losing money on horse races, then he needed to talk to her about money management.

For goodness' sake, he had a business degree from the University of Georgia. He knew a little something about the matter.

Since it was Sunday afternoon, the track was fairly crowded. Dan parked and went in, keeping an eye on Dixie the entire time.

She stopped at the entrance to the VIP area, and after a few moments, she was allowed in. It wasn't private box seating like at the opera or Sanford Stadium. It was open for all to see.

Dan took a seat where he didn't have to turn his head too far to keep an eye on her. She wore her Sunday best, a conservative white dress with blue flowers and blue pumps. The dress was neither low cut nor above the knee, and the modest coverage made her hourglass figure more attractive.

After sitting beside a guy who fit the stereotype for a bookie, she reached into her purse and passed him a small envelope. The guy's burgundy polyester suit fit him quite snugly, and his hair was slicked back with what Dan assumed was pomade, but it might have just been dirty.

His top lip sure looked dingy, but it was probably supposed to be a mustache. The popularity of Magnum P.I. made many men attempt the look women loved. Never mind the fact most men didn't resemble Tom Selleck in the least or possess his ability to grow a full mane on his upper lip.

If the greasy guy with the dirty lip had an Indian name, it would be Beaver Shadow Lip. Dan could almost hear his grandpa's laugh.

The beaver's smirk turned upside down when he counted the money. Bookies were supposed to like money, so something about the scene appeared wrong.

He spoke to Dixie, and she shook her head and said something back to him. When she stood to go, he grabbed her arm.

Dan got to his feet, and before he knew it, he pushed past the supposed security guy. When he saw Dan coming, he basically stepped out of the way.

"Let me go," Dixie was saying to the beaver.

"Hey, darlin'. There you are." Dan put his arm around her, slapping the beaver's arm away at the same time. "I thought you were gonna wait for me."

Dixie was shaking, and seeing her so frightened made his vision blur red.

"Oh." The beaver turned away, appearing disinterested. "I didn't know you'd moved on so quickly. It was a pleasure doing business with you, Mrs. Johnson. Consider this the end of our dealings."

The man never glanced their way again, as far as Dan could tell. Part of him wished the beaver would've put up a fuss, but it seemed self-preservation was the better part of valor, in his case.

When Dan got Dixie to her car, she burst into tears.

He wrapped his arms around her. "You wanna tell me what that was all about?"

"What are you doing here?" She pounded his chest once with her palms.

He explained himself.

"I was so afraid to come here today." She wiped her eyes with his handkerchief and told him about her late husband's gambling debt and the payoff. Then she cried some more.

"It's all right, darlin'. Big Dan's here." He glided his hands across her back.

She pulled away and her red-rimmed blue eyes glowed. "Don't you see? I'm so ashamed. I never wanted you or anyone else to know about this. Especially not my girls."

"Darlin', your secret's safe with me." He used his thumb to brush under her eye. "It's over now.

Isn't it?"

"I hope so." She inhaled a shaky breath. "I was afraid he was gonna ask for more."

"If he ever hassles you again, I want you to come to me, and I'll take care of it. Promise me, Dixie."

"I can't. It's not your problem." She set her jaw into a determined look he'd come to recognize.

"That's a damn lie. You work for me. I care about you and your girls. That makes it my problem. Get that through your pretty head, all right?"

He had a hand on either side of her face, so she couldn't turn away. "I'll follow you back to your house. I want to see the girls."

He kissed the center of her forehead.

Chapter Twelve

Dixie spent most of the drive back to her house watching Dan follow her in the rearview mirror and replaying their conversation in her head.

When he'd said he wanted to see the girls, she had half-smiled and asked, "Will you think I'm a bad mother if I punished them last night?"

His straight-from-a-romance-novel reply before he opened her car door and helped her in had been, "I don't think you have a bad bone in your body. You're too good to be true."

She kept shaking her head. It was the exact thought she'd had about him when she'd heard his voice and felt his protective arm around her at the track. Eddie had been on the verge of explaining how good they would be together. At least, he'd asked her out and not forced her into something.

A shudder ran though her.

At home, she parked and waited for Dan to join her. They followed the noise and found the girls in the backyard. Liz sat on the back steps, playing guitar, and the younger girls were taking turns jumping on the trampoline.

"Mr. Dan, Mr. Dan." Katie and Maddie rushed to see who could get to him first.

He knelt down to their eye level. "I see you ladies survived your punishment."

"Yes, sir," Katie said. "Mama gave us the choice to get switched or no trampoline for a week."

"We took the switch," Maddie said. "It hurts, but when it's over, you can play again."

"My boy opted for the same, but he got the belt. Aunt May's known to use a switch on them from time to time though."

"Did you come to watch me jump?" Maddie raced back to the trampoline, her stuffed horse tight in her clutches.

"Absolutely," he said.

"You can say no," Dixie told him.

"What? And miss out on all that cuteness bouncing in the air?" He grinned and followed after Maddie and Katie.

Dixie excused herself to change clothes, not wanting to ruin one of her few dresses by playing outside in it. She didn't get new clothes very often because three growing girls had more needs than she did.

Thankfully, Nancy's daughter, Sheila, was a clothes horse. She was two years older than Liz, so she happily handed down her old things when she got new ones. Liz would go through Sheila's clothes and pass them on to Katie and so on.

The problem Dixie was having was Liz grew

taller every day, and keeping her in jeans without her looking like she was expecting a flood was a challenge.

Shoes were another expense because the girls wore them out in no time at all. She often got their sneakers from the dollar store or TG&Y.

The younger girls hadn't yet learned to complain about it, but Liz noticed the other kids at school wore Keds. She might have been okay with the off-brand if the class bully hadn't pointed it out in front of everyone.

Dixie didn't want her girls to be materialistic, but she did want to give them the best of everything. She supposed all parents wanted the same for their children. Working for Dan and no longer having Steve's gambling debts hanging over her head would free up some money, so she could do more for them.

The prospect excited her as she shimmied into her faded Levi's.

When she returned to the back stoop, Dan and Liz were seated on the step, talking about their favorite bands. The younger girls were jumping together, which was never a good idea. Someone usually got hurt.

"Mr. Dan, look at us," Maddie called out about the time Katie boinged her off the trampoline, sending her flying through the air.

Maddie landed straddling the springs, getting pinched. She cried out as Katie tried to help her.

Dixie ran to get her little one off of the dangerous piece of equipment. "Katie, baby, back away."

Dan lifted Katie off of the trampoline, but that caused the springs to clamp down on the tender skin of Maddie's inner thigh, making her squall louder.

Dixie pressed the mat to release the coil while she lifted Maddie into her other arm. Dan took her from Dixie, carried her inside, and laid her on the couch.

"Liz, go get the tackle box," Dixie said. "Maddie, baby, open your legs, so I can check."

She shook her head and cried. "I don't want Mr. Dan to see my panties."

"He's not going to look at your panties, baby. He just wants to make sure you're okay."

Dan knelt near her head and brushed her hair from her forehead. "I'll look at your pretty face, sugar, so your mama can fix you up. I'm not too good with injuries as you probably remember from Paul's accident yesterday."

Maddie sniffled. "Is he better?"

His big thumb rubbed the back of Maddie's hand while Dixie parted her legs and examined her inner thigh.

"It's scabbing over, and he says it feels stiff and sore. I gave him some aspirin to help with the pain."

"Ow, Mama, ow!" Maddie jerked and screamed.

Dan cradled her to his chest, his eyes desperate. The burglar bars Dixie had placed over her heart officially fell off.

"I'm sorry, baby." Dixie used a soothing tone. "You got pinched good in two places, and it made little blisters. The ointment will help, but I had to touch the spots to apply it. I'll put bandages on, and it'll feel better soon."

When Dixie was finished, Dan picked Maddie up and sat on the couch, rocking her while her tears dried. "That broke my heart slap in two."

"We're gonna have to make a new rule," Dixie said. "No jumping in skirts or short pants."

"It was my fault, Mama," Katie said. "We weren't supposed to jump at the same time. I broke the rule. I'm sorry, Maddie." She reached in the little pink purse she carried everywhere and pulled something out. "You can wear some of my lipstick."

Dixie tried not to laugh.

Nancy and Sheila gave Katie their old lipsticks and other makeup. She had a shoebox full of it. Katie's favorite past time was putting on makeup and practicing on Maddie since Liz wouldn't let her experiment on her face.

Dan chuckled. "A little lipstick will fix you right up, sugarfoot."

"I have to check Katie every morning before I put her on the bus to make sure she isn't wearing makeup." Dixie contained her laughter.

"I thought her lips looked a little pink at the party yesterday. Would you ladies like to go get some ice cream?"

"That'll make me feel better, Mama." Maddie sniffed.

A short time later, they sat at the Dairy Queen eating sundaes. Maddie clung to Dan like the chocolate ice cream clung to her chin.

"Uncle Ben Hill's getting the pool ready this

week," Dan said. "If you girls aren't busy next Saturday, you can come help the boys christen it."

The younger girls oohed and aahed until Liz spoke up. "We have our dance recital next Saturday."

"Ooh, Mr. Dan, you can come see us dance." Katie nearly bounced out of her chair.

"Girls," Dixie said. "Mr. Dan already has plans to swim with his boys next Saturday. He can't come to your dance recital."

Liz laughed as Dan let out a sigh of relief. "You looked like a deer in headlights, Mr. Baker."

"Well, then," he said. "Put it on your calendar for the following Saturday. That's the employee barbeque, so everyone's coming with their kids to swim and eat."

"Can we, Mama?" Katie asked expectantly.

Dixie had vowed not to take her girls back to Southland because they'd caused so much trouble on their first visit. It was so hard to say no to those excited little faces though.

She sighed. "I'll think about it."

***

Dan and the boys spent Saturday morning in the pool. Then he dragged them, kicking and screaming, to a dance recital. The younger boys mostly complained about the ties he made them wear; whereas, Danny complained about wasting two hours of his life watching a bunch of girls in sparkly costumes.

"You boys remember your mama was a dancer when I met her? I went to see her dance in a performance or two." *Or twenty, more like*. Once she'd stolen his heart, he couldn't not support her.

"She used to dance with us," Johnny said. "The walls."

"The waltz." Dan squeezed Johnny's shoulder. "She used to dance with me, too."

He had been a no-account country boy with yuppie aspirations when they'd met at UGA. She was the debutante. He was the fraternity boy, trying to figure out who he wanted to be. Ella helped refine him to the point where he could mix with her family and society friends—all while letting him know he didn't have to change his basic values to be accepted by the upper crust. A little polish and shine was all he'd needed.

"I guess it'll be okay to watch girls dance," Danny said. "I'll do it in memory of Mama."

"That's mighty big of you." Dan pursed his lips as his son's words rolled around in his mind. "I think."

After accepting programs, they walked into the auditorium, and Dan spotted Dixie, front and center, seated next to Nancy. He walked down the aisle and sat beside her.

Dixie was looking away from him, so Nancy saw him first. "Fancy seeing you here, Dan Baker."

Dixie jerked her head around, her mouth hanging open. "Wha-what are you doing here? And you dragged the boys along? Poor things. Hey, boys."

"Hey, Miss Dixie," they said in unison.

"We couldn't let the girls down and miss their big show." He winked.

"The girls will be thrilled, but I can't believe

you would subject yourself to this. It'll be torture for your boys."

"They're interested in seeing what their mama used to do when she was young."

She nodded and blinked, her eyes glistening. He reached into his back pocket and handed her his handkerchief.

"Thank you." She dabbed at her eyes.

He wanted to put his arm around her, but in such a public place, it would start the rumor mill spinning. It might ruin Dixie's good name if folks thought she was getting cozy with her boss.

He really should have thought this through a little more, but he hadn't considered it beforehand.

Danny wouldn't be the only one calling her a gold-digger if word got out and they were seen together too often. Dan knew better, but Dixie's feelings may get hurt if people started to talk.

After the recital, he and the boys waited to say hello to the girls, and then Dan planned to head home.

Kicking himself because he should have brought them flowers, he felt his cheeks grow warm. His brain was not firing on all cylinders. He was amazed it worked at all when he was in close proximity to Dixie. He hadn't been around females in so long, he'd forgotten what they liked and how to treat them.

"Dan," Nancy said. "We're taking the girls to Shoney's if you fellas would care to join us."

"Hey, Mr. Dan." Katie and Maddie wrapped their arms around his legs.

He was a goner. He squatted in front of them.

"I've never seen such pretty dancers in all my days."

"I saw you from the stage," Katie said. "You waved at me."

"I didn't know you could see me, doll."

Johnny opened a brown sack he'd been carrying. "I brought y'all a present."

Dan thought he'd brought comic books to read during the recital. Instead, Johnny pulled out three Rubik's Cubes and gave one to each of Dixie's girls.

His face turned red as he looked at Nancy's daughter. "I'm sorry I don't have one for you."

"It's okay. I have one already," Sheila said.

"I think we're going to head home for dinner," Dan said.

"But, Daddy," Paul pulled on his sleeve, "I want one of those chocolate fudge cakes."

"Those are my favorite," Liz said.

"Me too," all the kids chimed in.

So much for going home.

Chapter Thirteen

Glancing up from her desk, Dixie locked eyes with Dan. He lounged against the door jamb like he owned the place. Well, he did own the place, but still, it was her office.

She put on her mental armor, since he was probably there to hound her about the company picnic at Southland. Everyone at the office was talking about it, and when they asked Dixie if she was going, she gave a noncommittal response.

Dan had gone as far as to enlist her girls to encourage her until she gave in.

"Have you got a sec?" He wore a serious expression.

She leaned forward in her chair, nerves jangling. "Sure."

He took the empty seat across the desk from her. "It might look bad if you're the only one who doesn't come to the party. It could make you look guilty of something."

Her face heated. "I *am* guilty of something. And after our last visit, I don't trust my girls not to embarrass me...or burn down your house."

"You have nothing to feel guilty about." He slanted his head to one side. "Are you ever going to stop beating yourself up about that night? Because it wasn't all you."

"I know, but seeing you every day doesn't make it easy to forget what happened."

A slow smirk drew up one corner of his mouth. "Are you saying I'm unforgettable?"

Before Dixie could respond, the intercom buzzed. "Ms. Johnson, there's a Dr. Flint calling for you."

"Thanks, Betty Jo." She glanced at Dan. "Excuse me a minute." She picked up the receiver and tried to mimic Liz's telephone voice. "Hi, Dr. Flint."

"Call me Ron," he said. "Now that we're not working together, we don't have to be so formal. Did you talk to your new boss about the conference?"

"Not yet, but I will." Keeping her eyes down, she twirled a pen in her fingers.

"I made copies of the program information and registration form for you. I can drop them by your office later. Are you free for lunch?"

"Um, I have a working lunch today..."

Dixie briefly lost her train of thought as Dan shifted in his seat. His big body radiated power, and she swore the room got warmer.

"Ah, if you want to drop the paperwork off though, the secretary can get it to me. I appreciate it, Doc—I mean, Ron."

"Hold on, missie. Are you available for lunch another day, another week? I know your husband hasn't been dead quite a year, but I always got the feeling you two weren't that close."

Her neck was on fire, and she tucked her chin to check how red her chest was above the top button of her shirt. "Um, I can't talk right now. My boss is here."

"I'll try you later." Dr. Flirt's voice held a hint of a promise.

"Okay, goodbye." It took her two tries to hang up because she missed the cradle the first time. Being scrutinized made her anxious.

Dan leaned back in his chair and raised an eyebrow. "Ron? Dr. Flint? What did he want besides to take you out to lunch?"

Dixie fanned herself with a manila folder and told him about the medical conference.

"We should go," he said.

She furrowed her brows. "We?"

"It'll be research for the new division. And in Las Vegas? That place is one big party. Don't you need a working vacation? Time away from the girls since they embarrass you so much and you can't take them anywhere?"

She stopped fanning and gave him the mom look. "Now you're just being facetious. Tell me why you stopped by again."

"To let you know that if you don't come to the pool party and wear a bathing suit, I'll fire you." He threaded his fingers before he put his hands behind his head.

"You can't do that." Her eyes were glued to the expanse of pectoral muscles straining against the fabric of his shirt.

"I think I can. The sign on my door says Big Boss."

***

Dan had only been kidding about firing Dixie, but she'd relented. He probably shouldn't have insisted on the bathing suit because as soon as she took off her oversized T-shirt to reveal a fitted one-piece, his body woke up.

Hell, it'd been awake since the night they got stuck. Her nearness always caused testosterone to flood his system. It was not a good time to have a serious reaction with all of his employees and their families bearing witness.

Look away, he told himself, but his eyes were glued to the details they'd missed in the dark backseat of his Blazer. His hands had touched her, but seeing was believing.

Someone called his name, and he forced himself to turn away and wave to the newly arriving guests.

When Dan surveyed the scene again, all of the men were trying not to stare at Dixie. He picked up her T-shirt from the chair where she'd tossed it and strode to edge of the pool where she sat with her feet in the water.

Sitting next to her, he handed her the shirt. "I'm afraid I'm going to have to ask you to put this back on."

"Am I blinding everyone with my ghostly white skin?" She slid it over her head.

"Something like that." He glanced around. "I'm actually trying to save you from making enemies with the womenfolk." *And saving myself from public humiliation.*

She furrowed her brow. "What do you mean?"

"Jealousy can be an ugly green monster."

And didn't he know it? The monster had reared its head when Dan saw the looks Dixie was getting from the male contingent. He'd considered firing them all until the logical part of his brain rejoined the reasoning process. Another thought he'd had was to beat his chest and yell, "Mine!" Again, letting his hormones control him would be unwise.

"I'm sorry. I didn't think…Um…" A flush ran up her neck to her cheeks.

"Don't worry about it, dah-Dixie." He clenched his fist to stop from patting her bare knee and instead shook his head. It was damn near impossible not to touch her or call her his pet name.

Just then, Danny and his best bud, Jason, walked by.

"Her tits are as big as the girls in our grade," Jason said. "She should be in a bikini instead of a one-piece."

"Excuse me." Dan got up to go beat a kid.

The only young girl he could've been talking about was Liz. And while he loved Jason like a son, he also had protective feelings for Liz, heck, for all of Dixie's girls.

"Jason Powell. Come here, boy."

The boys stopped and turned to face him.

"I have a bone to pick with you." Dan took a threatening step forward.

"Uh-oh," Danny said. "You're in trouble about something."

"Sir?" Jason's voice trembled as he stepped backward.

"It's impolite to talk about a woman's bits in mixed company."

"I didn't say bits, I said—"

"I know what you said. Her mama heard you say it, too."

Jason had the decency to blush. "I'm sorry. Should I apologize?"

"I think it'd be best if you said nothing else on the matter. It's disrespectful to say things like that about women."

"Why? I meant it as a compliment. She looks good for a twelve-year-old."

Dan huffed out a breath. "Jason, I know you boys are at that age where you're starting to notice girls, but she's too young. Stop noticing her. Look at girls your own age or better yet, older ones."

"Her mama looks—"

"If you like your nose in the center of your face, you better not finish that statement." Dan rested his fists on his hips.

"Sorry, gosh. I guess she's too old for me to look at." Jason kept his eyes downcast, but a tinge of sarcasm laced his voice.

Dan caught the growl low in his throat before it escaped. "The Johnson women are off limits. Don't look at any of them."

"Why do you care so much, Dad?" Danny asked.

"Because I happen to respect all of them, and if

I hear someone disrespect them, I'm gonna take issue with that." He directed his attention back and forth between them. "You get me?"

Both boys nodded. "Yes, sir."

"Part of your job as a man is to protect women and children from harm. Even words can cause damage. If you want to act like a real man, remember that." He paused and turned to Jason. "If I hear anything disrespectful from you again, I'm gonna take you to the woodshed."

"Trust me, Jace. You do not want to go there," Danny said.

Chapter Fourteen

Dixie left the side of the pool and asked Liz to keep an eye on her sisters. Going to the chair where she'd piled their clothes, she put her shorts back on, wishing she could run and hide after Dan called her out in front of everyone.

He hadn't been loud about it, just matter of fact. Everyone saw him hand her the T-shirt and ask her to put it on. The last thing she wanted was to outshine anyone or call attention to herself, but people who didn't know her might think she was trying to get the boss's notice.

She had certainly noticed him with his broad chest and muscled arms. She hadn't realized he had so much chest hair.

When she recalled their night together, she wasn't surprised. A vague memory of her brushing it with her fingers warmed her from the inside out.

It was dark and she'd been drinking. It'd been *wham, bam, thank you, ma'am.*

Well, not the second time. But in the grand scheme of things, their short time together was a drop in the mud.

Dixie shuffled her feet, unsure where to turn now that she was covered.

Miss May came out of the back door, carrying a tray of food in each hand.

Dixie headed her way. "Can I help?"

"You sho' can. There's 'bout ten gallon jugs of sweet tea inside on the table."

Dixie went in and carried four of them out at once then returned for another load. Dan caught her on her second trip.

"Give me those, woman." He took the four jugs from her.

After returning for the last two, she met him at the drink station. Beside the table sat the largest ice cooler she had ever seen. If it were empty, she could probably fit inside the thing.

"Dixie, shug," May said. "Will you start putting ice in cups and pouring tea, so they'll be waiting when the folks come by with their plates?"

"I'd be glad to."

"She likes you," Dan whispered. "She wouldn't let anyone else help."

Working at the beverage table put Dixie in a position to speak to almost everyone at the party. She tried to smile and be pleasant. Most people were kind in return. One or two of the wives whom she'd never met gave her the cold shoulder. She shrugged it off, but they would be the ones to start the gossip.

From her vantage point, she had a good view of

the barn. Danny and his friend Jason went in and exited a few minutes later.

After a little time passed, she saw them go back in with a couple of the teenagers and Liz.

Dixie left an open gallon of tea sitting out, so people could help themselves. Something was afoot in the barn, and she intended to check it out.

She squeezed in the small opening left between the barn door and the jam and glanced around. Laughter rang out from the hay loft, so she quietly climbed the ladder.

She found the kids passing a couple of beer cans around. The cooler which sat open between them gave her flashbacks from the night she'd met Big D.

"Have those beers turned rancid yet?" she asked.

Thuds resounded as cans hit the floor and kids stood, arms up to show their innocence. She liked busting them and seeing all those wide eyes and mouths. There were a few seconds when their fate hung in the balance, and she got to decide what it would be.

"Please don't tell my dad," Danny pleaded.

"You trying to corrupt my daughter, Danny Baker?" She put a hard edge in her voice and gave the impression of looking down her nose at him although she was below his eye level.

"No, ma'am." Danny shook his head.

"Maybe it was your friend, Jason, who thought it'd be a good idea to invite a twelve-year-old up for a beer." Dixie titled her head and raised her eyebrows at the young man in question.

"Mama!" Liz protested.

"Are you of legal age to drink alcoholic beverages, Elizabeth Ann? Are any of you?"

A chorus of *no, ma'ams* were followed by pleas for mercy.

She climbed all the way up and stepped to the side of the ladder. "All of you, get back to the pool area and stay there. One, two,…"

She struggled to contain her smile as the kids scrambled past her, down the ladder, and out the barn door. The commotion alone would draw their parents' attention.

Dixie walked over to the cooler to find one lone beer can, floating in a few cubes of ice and a lot of water. She reached in, picked it up, and popped the top.

Plopping down on a hay bale, she reclined a little and took a sip. It'd be better to hang out up here for the rest of the party than to return and face the whispers.

She leaned her head back and closed her eyes for a minute.

Inhaling the familiar scent of manure took her back to her childhood. It didn't stink. Instead, it was like coming home. The barn had been her favorite place, where her dad had taught her all about horses.

"Who do I need to take to the woodshed?"

Opening her eyes, she beheld the glorious vision of a shirtless Dan Baker resting at the top of the ladder. She took another sip of beer before she offered it to him.

He stalked toward her like a hungry animal and

took the can.

Something clinched deep inside, and she wanted the world to disappear for a moment, so she could relive bliss with the man she now knew had a heart of gold.

She shook herself mentally and stood. Thinking like that would get her in trouble.

Dan blocked her escape, watching her while he swallowed the beer and handed it back to her. She took the can, trying to distract herself with it, but his gaze was penetrating. Heat spread through her body, and her chest grew heavy with need.

Arching her back, she leaned toward him a little before she backed off. "I should go." She handed him the beer and stepped around him.

He caught her before she got to the ladder. "Don't leave yet, darlin'. If you want to discipline Liz privately, take her in the house, but don't go. Please."

The longing, the desire, the pleading note in his voice, all encouraged her to agree to stay.

She nodded once, staring into his eyes. Her mind cried, *kiss me*, but her mouth said, "Wait a few minutes before you come out. It might look bad if we exit together."

"I'm not going anywhere. I've got a beer to finish." He held up the can and waggled his eyebrows.

Every day, Dan was becoming more and more someone she wanted but couldn't have. Someone she didn't want to live without.

***

Dan did his best to ignore the sinking feeling in

his chest when Dixie piled her kids into the car and left in a parade of taillights with all of the others. In vain, he'd tried to get her to stay, but she was correct in reminding him of the favoritism it might reflect.

When the last car pulled away, Dan started toward the lake on the back of his property since there was a little daylight left. Before he'd cleared the back of the house, something on the steps caught his eye.

The stuffed horse had seen better days, but he smiled as he picked it up.

Hope filled his heart as he wished Dixie would turn her car around and come back for it. The telephone ringing drew him to the back door.

"Big Dan," Aunt May called. "Everyone gone?"

"Yeah. That Dixie?" He stepped toward the phone.

"Yep. She stopped in town. Realized they're missing part of the family." May passed him the receiver.

He cleared his throat but couldn't remove the smile from his voice. "Spike the Horsey is crying because sugarfoot abandoned him."

"Sugarfoot is crying because she's just realized he's missing. I'm calling from the payphone at the Piggly Wiggly. Would it be all right if we ran back to get him?"

"Absolutely, but you don't have to run. Y'all stay and help us eat some of these leftovers."

"Dan, I don't think—"

"Don't argue. Get your beautiful self back out

here in a jiffy. I want to show you something."

Dan was waiting with Horsey when they pulled up. He met them at the car and gave Maddie her toy.

"You girls go on in the house. Aunt May's making you plates, and the boys are about to eat. I'm taking your mama for a walk."

He grabbed Dixie's hand and tugged. She tried to resist, but he wasn't having it. He towed her down to the lake.

The sun was getting low in the sky and shadows danced around the wooded shoreline.

Her steps slowed as she surveyed the scene, her lips slightly parted. "This is beautiful, Dan." She took another step and dropped his hand before she turned in a full circle. "Magical. You've got a little piece of heaven here at Southland."

"It's home." He moved behind her and pushed her hair over one shoulder, exposing her slender neck.

"Dan—" Her body stiffened.

Unable to resist, he kissed her nape.

She shivered as she inhaled sharply then leaned into him. He wanted to remove everything covering her and use his lips to explore every part of her.

Grabbing the bottom of her T-shirt, he pulled it up and over her head as she raised her arms. He glided his hands down her sides and kissed her shoulder next to the strap of her one-piece.

"This is the place where you can come swim anytime and not have to worry about what anyone thinks of you in your suit." *But I'd really like to get you out of it.*

His hands skimmed her waist as he reached around her and unbuttoned her cutoff jeans, pushing them down her hips.

Power surged through him when she yielded. He could have her again, and she desired him too. But the timing and the lack of privacy made him rethink his plan of seduction.

"Come on." He took her hand and walked into the water.

"Whew, it's a little cool." Her skin pricked with chill bumps.

"You'll warm up when you start swimming." He dove under and swam away from shore, the cool water calming the fire which had built inside him.

After he popped up for air, she swam toward him. When she was within reach, she turned on her back to float.

"How do you do that?" He treaded water next to her.

"Granny Bite taught me when I was young. Floating is an art."

"It is when you do it, darlin'." He leaned back to try it.

After sinking to the bottom, he surfaced to find her pointing toward the shore near where they'd entered the water.

"I know it might ruin the landscape of the place, but if you put a dock right over there—"

"Ha." He cut her off. "I was just about to tell you I'm putting a dock there this summer. The boys will love diving from it and swimming out here." He paused. "Your girls too, if you bring them."

"You're too good to us, Dan. You might spoil

us with all this attention." Her expression made it seem like that might not be a good thing.

"That's what I'm trying to do. You deserve to be spoiled."

She ducked her chin, concealing her smile. The shy gesture sent another surge of longing through his veins.

They moved to shallower water and stood.

Throwing caution out the window, he pulled her close until their bodies pressed against each other. As he lowered his lips to hers, the kids broke through the tree line, talking loudly.

Dixie dove under as the boys ran and splashed into the lake.

"What're y'all doing out here, Daddy?" Paul gurgled and treaded water next to them.

"Miss Dixie didn't get to swim today, so I brought her out here to give her a chance."

"Mama, can we come swim too?" Katie asked.

Dan glanced over at Dixie, who had resurfaced and looked as if she was about to say no. "Come on. Let the girls swim."

Her shoulders sagged. "All right."

With all eight of them frolicking together in the water, Dan had a profound sense of something he'd been missing.

He'd found home again.

These girls needed a father, and he needed them. Especially their mama. Convincing her would take a miracle, so it was a good thing he had an angel on his side.

Chapter Fifteen

On Monday, Dixie peered up from her desk to find Dan in the doorway, spying on her again. A smart remark about him installing a camera in her office was on the tip of her tongue, but he could afford to do it and probably would if she gave him the idea. *Pervert*.

She stifled a laugh and pretended to finish what she was working on.

When she'd made him wait long enough, she gave him her full attention. "How can I help you?"

"What did you do to punish Lizabelle for drinking beer with the boys?" His arms were crossed over his broad chest.

"She says she never actually got to taste it, but I took her guitar away for a week anyway, just for being coerced into a barn with the promise of beer."

"I took Danny's stereo out of his room after I took him to the woodshed. He's pissed."

"Poor kid's not gonna have any skin left on his

rump if you keep taking him to the woodshed."

She wrinkled her nose. "I'm kinda sorry I followed the kids, but I knew they were up to something. And after I heard what Jason said about Liz, I couldn't take any chances."

"You did the right thing, darlin'. Someone needed to keep an eye of them. I'm sorry they tried to corrupt Liz." His dark eyes held sincerity.

Dixie didn't often get the chance to share parenting woes, and she couldn't let the opportunity pass. "You know, she's the child I rarely have to discipline. She's my rule follower, and as soon as she realizes she's done something wrong, she usually admits it and asks for forgiveness. I feel like I punish the little ones all the time and Liz hardly ever."

"She's mature and wise beyond her years." His body rocked as his head nodded.

Why did she have to be so aware of the space he filled? Why did she want him nearer?

"The Lord knows she's a lot smarter than I am. She scores genius on those IQ tests, but I've never fully explained that to her. They put her in a special class at school to challenge her with upper level work. She barely bats an eye at anything they put in front of her."

He moved a little further into the room, leaning his back against the wall. "What about her guitar? Is that easy for her?"

"That's a little more of a struggle, and she works at it a lot, trying to figure it out on her own. I think that's why she enjoys it." Dixie shrugged.

"She *is* special. I knew it the first time I talked

to her on the phone. It can't be easy to parent a genius. Of course, I think all of your girls are special, each in her own way."

Dixie's heart swelled at the affection in his voice. "I can say the same about your boys. They're a chip off the old block. Handsome, intelligent, charming, and sweet as pie."

"Hmm. That's quite a compliment. Thank you, dah-Dixie." He stepped closer and sat on the edge of the guest chair. "Did anyone say anything to you at the party or did you hear any talk here at work today?"

"About what?" she asked, although she knew exactly what he meant.

"Nothing." He shook his head. "If anyone says anything inappropriate or hurts your feelings, I want you to come to me."

"You want me to tattle, Big Boss? You want them to start calling me teacher's pet?" She leaned forward and jutted out her chin.

"No." His gaze swept down to her top button then back up to her eyes.

"Whatever happens, I'll deal with it unless it gets out of hand." Her voice was more confident than she actually felt.

"I don't want anyone to get away with thinking they can badmouth you."

"Why? What's makes me so special? Would you do the same for Betty Jo?"

"I don't have to do it for her. You're special because you were brought in to head up a new division that no one else knows much about. The secrecy of the situation causes speculation." He didn't admit the attraction between them might be obvious to anyone with eyes.

She couldn't let it slide. "They think you wanted to put your mistress on the payroll?"

"Who knows what they think about me?" He furrowed his brow and pursed his lips. "Wait. Did someone say you were my mistress?"

"No." *Yes*, she said silently. "I know what they think of you, Dan. They've known you and worked for you for a long time, so they love and respect you. Let's just give them a little while to get to know me and accept me."

"When we launch this thing, you're going to blow their minds." His grin lit up his face, and his assurance left her with no doubt.

She didn't want the credit though. "This is your brainchild, Dan, and you deserve any accolades that come from it."

"You're my partner in this. I had to have the right person, and you're it. I feel it in my bones."

"Thank you, sir. I'll do my best." She offered him a mock salute.

"Don't sir me, dah—"

Dixie cleared her throat and looked over Dan's head. "Hello, Charlie. Do you need to speak to me or with the Big Boss?"

***

Later in the week, Dan took some papers to Betty Jo for her to mail and walked in on a conversation.

"I'm sorry, sir," Betty Jo said to the man standing in front of her desk. "Miss Johnson had a family emergency and had to leave early. I can put the paperwork on her desk."

"Is everything okay?" the man asked.

"Sure is." Dan moved closer and extended his hand. "Dan Baker. And you are?"

"Dr. Ronald Flint. I'm here to drop something off for Dixie, and I had hoped she'd be free for lunch."

Dan let his superiority roll off him in waves. "Oh, the school called, and one of her girls is under the weather."

In truth, the school called because Maddie had head lice. Dixie had panicked because she'd had to cut the girls' hair short the last time it happened when they were much younger.

Dan had sent her home with enough hair treatment from the supply room to treat herself and the girls for a week if needed.

"Is this the information about the conference in Las Vegas?" Dan reached for the folder Dr. Flint held.

"It is." He relinquished his hold. "If you decide to send Dixie, don't worry about sending her on her own. I'll be there, and she and I are old friends. We worked together for ten years at the hospital. I'll take good care of her."

I bet you will, Dr. Love.

Dan perused the papers while his mind raced. The man reminded Dan of the actor from Knight Rider with his dark permed hair and slick leather jacket. Dan bet he drove a fast car, too. Not a Trans Am though. Because he was a doctor, he'd need something showier.

Corvette, Dan guessed.

"They normally have a lot of vendors at these things, don't they?" he asked.

"They do. Your business would be a great addition."

"I'm glad you think so, Dr. Flint. Thanks for stopping by." Dan shook his hand again.

He leaned against Betty Jo's desk, and together they watched the doctor leave. Outside, he lowered himself into a fire-engine red Corvette.

"You aren't gonna let Dixie go anywhere unchaperoned with that guy, are you?" Betty Jo asked.

Dan pursed his lips. "There's not a snowball's chance in hell."

***

Since his hands were full with carry-out plates from the local soul food restaurant, Dan used his foot to tap on Dixie's front door.

"I figured y'all would be too busy to cook." He walked past Liz to the kitchen after she opened the door for him.

"Yes, sir. The stove is kind of in use at the moment."

A huge metal washtub filled with sheets and boiling water covered all four eyes of the stove top.

"Sure is. How you planning to empty that?"

Liz scratched her chin. "I was just contemplating that little problem. My first idea was to let the water cool down before I try to move it."

"Give me a couple of oven mitts, and I'll take care of it. You probably have more sheets to boil, don't you?" he asked.

"Yes, sir."

Dan picked up the heavy wash pan and dumped the water into the sink then took tongs from Liz to transfer the sheets into the washing machine.

Liz poured in bleach and started it up.

"How're you doing, honey?"

Liz smiled. "Fine. The school nurse checked me, and I'm okay." She paused a moment. "I guess since Katie and Maddie share a bed, they're both afflicted with the little buggers."

Chuckling, he pulled out a box of black trash bags from the supplies he'd brought. "You start the next set of sheets to boiling. I'll go bag up the pillows and toys."

"Thank you, Mr. Baker."

Before he headed to the back of the house, he gave Liz a hug and kissed the top of her head.

He paused at the open bathroom door where Dixie was bent over the tub with two crying little girls inside. Clearly, she was up to her eyeballs in lice shampoo with her T-shirt soaked through and water puddled beneath her knees.

A thousand sexy thoughts vied for his attention, but the strong medicinal smell of the hair treatment killed every one of them.

***

Dixie let out a scream and put a wet hand over her heart. The deep male voice had nearly given her a heart attack.

"I'm sorry to sneak up on you, darlin'. Get them rinsed and bring them to the living room, and I'll de-nit one of 'em for ya," Dan said.

There hadn't been a man past the kitchen of her house since Steve was alive. For a moment, she thought it'd been Steve, or his spirit rather, coming back to judge her for bad parenting, allowing their girls to get head lice. According to him, it had been her fault the time before when it'd happened.

Her heart still raced ninety to nothing.

Dan walked past the door again, carrying more black trash bags than she could count.

Lord, he had been in the bedrooms, maybe her bedroom. She tried to remember if she'd left her bra lying on the bed with her work clothes. She'd changed into ratty shorts and a T-shirt to tackle the lice situation and hadn't bothered to straighten up.

Worse than that, she was presently braless and her T-shirt was wet.

Despite everything, she was happy to see him.

When she forced her modesty aside, her eyes pricked with tears. He was here to help her. If Steve were alive, she still would have gotten to do this job on her own.

Dan's words from earlier in the week when he'd said she was his partner in the business venture had made her heart ache because it reminded her she'd never had a true partner in marriage.

She rinsed Katie's and Maddie's hair and got them out of the tub. Wrapping them in towels, she sent them to the living room while she snuck to her room for a dry shirt and a holder for her boulders.

"Looking for this?"

She turned to find him standing in the doorway, holding the bra which had been on the bed.

Unfortunately, the undergarment was more functional than it was pretty. Heat crept up her neck. His eyes fixed on her chest, and she crossed her arms in an attempt to cover up the excitement his nearness caused. Whether she wanted it to or not, her body always reacted around him.

He cleared his throat. "I wasn't sure if this could go in the wash. The girls were starving, so I told them to eat before we tackle the nits."

"Thanks." She reached out to take the bra from him.

He yanked it out of her reach. "I think I like you better without it."

She dipped her head in embarrassment.

"Aw, darlin', I'm sorry." His arms wrapped around her. "I know you're upset about the girls, and I was trying to distract you. I didn't mean to make it worse. I'm here to help. Tell me what you need."

Another night with you. She couldn't look him in the eye because the body parts she wanted to conceal were pressed against him. "I need my bra, on my body, in its proper place, so I don't feel like such a floozy in front of my boss."

"You weren't wearing a bra the night we met." He pulled back with a smirk dancing on his lips.

"I know. I was being a floozy."

His body shook with laughter. "You're welcome to be a floozy with me anytime, darlin'. I seem to remember enjoying the experience immensely."

Dixie had too, but telling him so might not be the best thing to do. "Thank you for coming to help me and for feeding my kids again. I'm starting to think you don't trust me to take care of them."

"That's not it at all, and you know it. Put your bra on so you can eat, too. You need your strength." He kissed her forehead and left her to her thoughts.

After supper, Dixie took Katie and the nit comb and got to work. Because of her lighter hair, the white nits were difficult to see.

Dixie couldn't believe Dan was sitting beside her working on Maddie's scalp.

"I hate the stigma that comes with lice," she said by way of conversation. "Most people assume the kids who get it are dirty, but lice aren't too picky about whose hair they crawl onto. In my experience, the cleaner the hair the more attractive it is to lice."

"There's something to that," he said. "All three of my boys got it when they were each in kindergarten from the sleeping mats they shared with the other kids. Aunt May says that colored kids don't get head lice because of the oils and conditioners they use. The lice can't get a grip, she says."

"That makes sense. I wonder if I get a crème conditioner and let the girls wear it a few hours… I'll call one of my friends to ask her what she uses."

"I'm way ahead of you, darlin'. There's a bag on the counter with the stuff Aunt May told me to get and shower caps. She says to put it on dry hair and let them sleep in it. Then wash it out in the morning. It's supposed to smother the lice."

"You're a lifesaver. Aunt May, too. I really appreciate your help." She couldn't stop the tears.

"Why are you crying, Mama?" Liz asked as she came over with a paper towel and dabbed at

Dixie's eyes.
"I'm a little overwhelmed, baby."
"Because of the lice?" Liz asked.
"Because of the man next to me."

Chapter Sixteen

Dan hadn't been able to come up with a good excuse to see Dixie over the weekend, and he was late getting into the office on Monday because he'd had to take Paul to the doctor about his asthma.

Nancy bumped into him on her way out from visiting Dixie. "We took an early lunch because of my court case. What are you and the boys doing this Saturday?"

"Nancy!" Dixie's voice held surprise and a warning.

"If I don't ask him, you never will. Listen Dan, Sheila and I were going to Six Flags with D and the girls on Saturday, but Sheila got invited to prom, so we have to bow out."

Dixie marched down the hall toward them. "Nancy, Dan and his crew and me and mine couldn't even get there in one vehicle anyway. Stop butting in."

"I have a Suburban," he said. "It's old, but it runs and seats nine."

"Well, there you go," Nancy said. "Problem solved. It's Katie's birthday present."

"Aw, the little doll's having a birthday?"

"Yeah," Dixie said. "She wanted to have a slumber party, but with the recent lice episode, no one's willing to let their daughters come over."

"Blasted idiots," he said. "Excuse me, ladies, but that really chaps my behind."

Dixie's eyes widened, and she pressed her lips together.

"What is it, D?" he asked.

She stared at the floor. "Nothing."

Dan could've sworn she was trying not to laugh.

"Uh-huh. I gotta go. Bye, Sister." Nancy kissed her cheek. "Bye, Dan." She waved her fingers in the air.

Dan walked Dixie to her office. "What's so funny?"

"It was what you said the first night I met you. After we…" She blushed.

"When I didn't know your name." He caressed her cheek with the back of his knuckles. "Well, I know it now. And I'll never forget it."

Early Saturday morning, Dan stopped in Bull Creek to pick up Dixie and the girls. His boys moved to the third row seat, and the ladies sat in the second row while Dixie joined him in the front.

"You didn't have to do this, Dan. But thank you for coming with us."

"My pleasure, darlin'."

When they were in Atlanta, minutes away from their destination, Liz said, "I've got a headache."

"Me too," Danny said. "I feel dizzy."

Dixie turned in her seat. "Johnny?"

"I think I have to throw up," Johnny said.

"Paul?" Dixie asked.

"He's asleep," Danny said.

"Wake him up.

Danny shook his brother and shouted his name. "He won't wake up."

"Dan, pull over."

"What is it?"

"Does this vehicle have a catalytic converter?"

"Not originally, but I had one put on it. Oh hell, are you thinking carbon monoxide?" He eased off to the side of the road but felt anything but easy.

Dan struggled to gain control of the fear gripping his heart.

Dixie opened the back door and took Paul as Danny passed him forward. "Get out of the car kids." She put Paul on the ground and started giving him breaths.

Not knowing what else he could do to help his children, Dan stood behind Johnny and rubbed his back as his son retched over the weeds. Gritting his teeth, Dan swallowed a howl of helplessness.

"He has a pulse," Dixie said. "How's Johnny?"

"Throwing up," Dan said. "What should we do?"

"We need to get Paul to the hospital."

It was chaos on the roadside as the girls huddled and prayed. Danny paced and cussed.

Johnny vomited, and Paul remained unconscious.

Dan's stomach sank to his toes, and the same feeling of doom he'd had when they'd gotten Ella's diagnosis nearly knocked him down. He had to take control.

He got to his feet, picking Johnny up as he stepped toward the SUV. "Danny, drive. Liz, put the girls in the front seat with you. Let down all the windows."

"I don't know how to get to the hospital," Danny said.

"I do," Liz said. "I'll navigate. Let's go, girls."

Dan held Johnny in the backseat with his head out the window while Dixie cradled Paul in her arms and gave him rescue breaths until they arrived at the hospital. Then they switched.

Dan stayed with Paul, and Dixie went with Johnny as the hospital staff took them into the Emergency Room. When Paul was on oxygen and the doctors assured Dan his son was okay, he went to the waiting room to check on the other kids.

Maddie sat in Danny's lap while Katie sat next to him, holding his hand. Liz paced. Danny looked miserable, but Dan wasn't sure if it was because his brothers were sick or the girls were all over him.

"Don't worry, Danny. They won't die," Maddie said. "I didn't hear the death knocks like when my daddy died."

Dan squatted in front of them. "What do you mean, sugarfoot? What are *the death knocks*?"

"You know," she said.

"Maddie," Liz said. "Mama doesn't want you to talk about that."

"I need to know, Lizabelle." Dan raised his gaze. "You can tell me, sugar."

"When someone's about to die, me and Mama hear a knock on the window. Sometimes, we see who it is. I saw my daddy riding a bull before he died."

"He hit a bull with his car and died," Katie explained.

"You saw that *before* his death?"

"Yes, sir. But I didn't know to warn him, so it's my fault he's dead." She hiccupped and started crying.

"No, sugar. It's not your fault." Dan lifted her from Danny's lap and held her close.

Danny stood as soon as he was free. "This is bullcrap."

"No, it's not, Danny," Katie said. "I believe them. Maddie has seen your mama, too."

"Liar."

"Danny, cut it out." Dan stopped his eldest with a pointed finger. "When did you see her, sugarfoot?"

"She took me to see the horses that day. She shut my mama in your office with you, too."

Dan remembered it as if it had just happened. Dixie had paled and her body shook, like she'd seen a ghost. She quit arguing about working for him and accepted the job.

Dixie came through the door. "Dan, Johnny's asking for you. How's Paul?"

"Fine, they put him on oxygen."

Dan headed past Dixie through the doors but stopped to turn back. He kissed her fast and furious then left her standing there open-mouthed and panting while he went to see his boy.

If he had any doubt before, it was gone. He was going to marry Dixie Johnson and adopt her daughters.

***

The sun shone brightly in a clear blue sky as Dixie leaned against her station wagon in the hospital parking lot and sighed.

"Thank y'all for bringing my car," she said to her brother and sister. "Dan says he's gonna torch the Suburban, and none of our kids are ever going to ride in it again."

"You said it had a catalytic converter installed," Larry said. "It's probably a bad connection. If you get me the keys, I'll take it to a mechanic friend of mine."

"I'll try, but I still don't think he'll take a chance with his boys. I wouldn't." *If I could afford to light my vehicle on fire.*

Dixie headed back into the hospital, her older siblings trailing her.

After both Johnny and Paul were released, Dan gave his keys to Larry, but Dixie knew deep down that beast of a car would never hold a Baker boy again.

Dan drove Dixie's car while both the younger boys sat in the front seat, Paul in her lap. Danny and the girls sat in the back with Maddie in Danny's lap.

Once at Southland, Dan carried Johnny and Dixie carried Paul up to their rooms. Danny and the girls followed in silence.

"Thank you for helping me," Paul said.

"You've got it anytime you need it, buddy." She brushed his hair back and kissed his forehead. "Thank you for being my brave boy and fighting with me. You're one tough kid."

His smile was all she needed to see.

As she was leaving his room, he said, "Goodnight, Mama D."

She stopped and glanced back.

He pulled the covers up to his chin and grinned. "My mama told me to call you that."

Dixie wasn't surprised. Being near the veil between this plane and the next, people often saw and heard things folks in this realm couldn't or wouldn't see.

"I love it." She winked. "Goodnight, cutie pie."

She turned from the door and slammed into a wall of hard muscle.

Dan's arms wrapped around her, and his lips pressed hard against hers. "Don't go anywhere. I need to talk to you," he said before stepping into Paul's room.

She was panicked to the point she almost walked past Johnny's room without telling him goodnight.

She needed to stop letting Dan kiss her. Why did he have to be so darn irresistible?

Slipping into his room, she sat on the bed next to Johnny. "Hey, sweetie, I'm so glad you're better."

"Me, too." His eyes widened.

Her fingers itched to pinch his little round cheeks. Intuition told her that as the middle child, he struggled to find his place and fit in, like her

Katie did. "You're a card. And so much like your dad."

"Really?" He beamed.

"Definitely." A prophetic word hit her. "You aren't going to have it as easy as your brothers, but you're going to have fun. And then one day, life will click, the right person, the right moment, the right time. You'll have it good, real good. The real thing, Johnny. But you have to be patient."

"How do you know?"

She shrugged. "I have a feeling. You're a good kid, and I love you." She kissed his forehead.

"Thanks, Mama D."

Dixie furrowed her brow but said nothing. It was catching, the name thing, and she was beginning to feel at home with these boys. Although, it wasn't really an option.

"Come on, girls." She walked past them at the top of the stairs, where they'd been waiting for her. "We need to go, so the boys can rest. Goodnight, Danny."

"G'night." And when she was almost out of earshot, he added, "Thank you."

Downstairs, she was stalled by Aunt May and Uncle Ben.

"It was a miracle from God that you were there Miss Dixie," Uncle Ben Hill said.

"Thank the Lawd," Aunt May said. "We glad you brought our boys back to us." She wrapped her arms tightly around Dixie.

"I know Dan's upset." Dixie pulled back and patted May's shoulder. "We'll just go, so they can all rest."

"Darlin'." The timbre of his voice as he spoke that one word made her insides turn to jelly.

She wanted to comfort the man who'd almost lost two of his sons, but her rational mind told her to run before she was in too deep.

Her heart knew it was already too late.

She turned and put one hand on Liz, the other on Katie, and Liz pulled Maddie close to her.

"I want to thank you girls," he said. "All of your prayers were answered, and my boys are well and sleeping in their own beds tonight."

"That's the best birthday present ever," Katie said.

"Don't you worry, doll baby. I'll make it up to you." He knelt in front of the girls and hugged them.

Dixie found her voice. "You don't have to do that."

"I know I don't have to, but I'm going to." He stood. "I owe you most of all."

Dixie flinched a little on the inside. If Dan was going to reward her, she'd rather it be out of love than recompense. She was glad she'd been there to help, but she didn't want him to feel an obligation to her.

"We'll go." Dixie employed her most polite tone. "I'll call tomorrow to check on the boys."

"Stay."

"We can't, but thank you and—"

"Dixie," he said. "Please stay."

She moved her hand from Katie's shoulder to his face. "No, Dan."

***

Monday morning, Dan rested his elbows on his desk and reminisced about watching Dixie's taillights disappear down the drive. Why had he ever thought she'd stay? He knew better.

Danny had come to stand by his side. "You gonna marry her, Dad?"

"Yep."

"I thought so. I just wanted to say you could do worse." Danny sighed. "I just wish she didn't come with so much baggage."

"That baggage is your sisters, and you don't know it yet, but one day, you'll claim them and defend them as if they were your blood."

"We'll see." Danny spun on his heel.

Dixie had called to check on the boys the next day, but she'd declined the invitation to spend the day at Southland. He didn't see her again until she showed up at his office door at the beginning of the workweek.

"I'm sorry to bother you so early with this, but I've hit a speed bump. It's been two weeks, and Senator Jenkin's office hasn't gotten back with me. It's the last thing we need for the application."

"Give me a minute." He flipped through his Rolodex and picked up the phone.

"Jimmy, it's Dan Baker. Someone from my office has been getting the runaround from somebody at yours."

"Big Dan, I apologize. I've been out of town. Listen, Martha and I are having a dinner party this Friday night at the Atlanta house. Sevenish. Come, bring a date, bring the paperwork, and I'll sign off on it."

Fool With My Heart

Dan looked Dixie over. It would be work to her, but it would be a date to him. He'd have to ease her into the idea of *going together*, much less down the aisle.

"I'll see you then, Jimmy." He hung up the phone and met her stare. "We're going to a dinner party at his place Friday night."

"That was Senator Jenkins on the phone?" Her eyebrows danced near her hairline.

"Yep." He wasn't sure what the big deal was.

Her head tipped to one side. "You call him Jimmy?"

He leaned back in his chair. "We're members of the same hunting club."

"Wow! Thanks for that." She turned to go.

"Do you have something to wear Friday night?"

"To a senator's house? Sure, I go places like that all the time."

He moved around the desk and took her hand. "Don't worry, darlin'. I'll call Nora Cook over at Cookie's Closet, and she'll fix you up."

"Do I have to go?" She looked at their hands and pulled hers away. "Can't you just go and get the signature?"

"I'm not going without you. They've been trying to fix me up with Martha's divorced sister since before Ella was cold in the ground. You go with me to get this thing signed, or we beat down another Congressman's door. The choice is yours." He hadn't meant to tell her the bit about the sister.

"I'm sorry about that, but do you think pretending I'm your date while I also work for you

141

is a good idea?"

"We won't be pretending." He gave her his most serious business face.

A streak of emotions flashed in her eyes in quick succession. The inner battle waging in her mind was written all over her face. And it might make him a total jerk, but it pumped him up. She belonged to him. All he had to do was claim her.

"Still, not a good idea." She turned to walk away.

"Stop worrying so much, darlin'. Go get a dress and look gorgeous, not that you have to try. I'll pick you up at six."

Chapter Seventeen

Dixie hadn't been able to eat all week, which made the dress she'd gotten from Nora Cook fit more loosely than it should have.

Her heart rate went from a trot to a gallop when the doorbell chimed. She hadn't been on a date in over fourteen years. Though she'd been trying to convince herself this was just business, the truth was blaring at her like the horn of an eighteen-wheeler.

The girls had been helping her get ready, but they ran to the door as soon as they heard Dan pull up. Between Liz laying out Dixie's undergarments, Katie offering makeup tips, and Maddie picking out the accessories, they had Dixie covered.

She put the earrings through her ears and slipped into her heels. Looking in the mirror, she took one long steadying breath before going to greet her escort.

Dan Baker in a suit was more delicious than

honey on a biscuit.

Dixie licked her lips and enjoyed watching him do the same as he took in her taupe sleeveless dress with black side panels and black pumps. The outfit made her feel sophisticated and worldly, even if she wasn't.

"Dixie, wow. There aren't words to describe how beautiful you look."

Her face warmed and she smiled. "Ditto."

"Girls, don't wait up." He winked, but his eyes didn't leave Dixie's face.

"We're going to bake a frozen pizza and watch movies, so we might be up late," Liz said.

"Nevertheless, good night, ladies." He kissed each of the girls on their cheeks.

"Night, girls." Dixie's heart smiled as her youngest girls hugged her hips. "I love you." She blew Liz a kiss.

"We love you too, Mama," Katie said.

"Have fun," Liz said.

Dan held out his arm. "Shall we?"

Dixie's mouth dropped open when she saw their ride. She'd only ever seen Dan in large vehicles. Tonight, he drove a Porsche 944 Silver Rose Edition, and Dixie's motor was running before he even started the car.

She liked to go fast.

He opened the door and helped her in. Her hemline rode up a little, but she didn't care. The leather seat hugged her almost as closely as any saddle ever had.

Dan slid behind the wheel. "You ready?"

She nodded.

He opened it up on the highway, and she leaned her head against the seat, closing her eyes.

"You okay?" His voice sent a chill along her skin.

"Yeah. Just trying to relax. I don't want to embarrass you."

"You won't. Do you like the car?"

"I *love* the car." *With a capital L.*

He smiled and shifted as he passed an old farm truck like it was standing still.

At the senator's house, Dan opened her door and lifted her out. Once she'd smoothed her dress, she rested her hand in the crook of his arm.

"Don't be nervous. You're just as good as any of them. And more beautiful."

"Spoken like someone who's walked a mile in my shoes."

"I don't want to walk anywhere in those shoes, darlin'. But they make your legs look phenomenal." He wriggled his eyebrows.

Heat shot straight to Dixie's toes. "Are you saying my legs don't look so good without the heels?"

"I didn't say that at all." His arm slid around her waist, his hand pressing firmly on her outer hip. "Your legs look great no matter what's on your feet."

The front door opened, and Dixie stood taller as Dan's hand glided to her lower back. He introduced her to Martha Jenkins and the Georgia State Senator himself.

"Welcome," they said in unison. "Come in."

Dixie's smile overstretched her mouth, as

anxiety churned her stomach. She and Dan followed their hosts through the marble lined foyer into the library.

The opulence of the rich mahogany and velvet accents was downplayed, not by the tuxedo-shirted bartender at the bar, but by the presence of a slushy machine.

"This is brilliant." The senator swept his arm out in an imitation of Barker's Beauties from *The Price Is Right*. "Instant margaritas. Tequila included."

The bartender poured a glass, and the host offered it to Dixie.

"Thank you, Senator."

"Call me Jimmy. Any friend of Big Dan's is a friend of mine." He raised his glass.

Heat crawled up her neck, and she sipped the drink, allowing the sweet, yet tart, lime flavor to momentarily distract her.

When she realized all eyes watched her in anticipation, she blurted out an obligatory response, "Delicious."

Dan winked, and as she drank, the warmth of his hand on her back began to do its job of calming her while he made small talk.

The only person who didn't seem happy to see Dixie was Martha's sister. Dixie hoped the lady's disappointment in Dan bringing a date wouldn't come back to bite them in the ankle. And being on the receiving end of glaring eyes was not how Dixie wanted to spend the evening.

With Dan glued close to her side, Dixie found the courage to pretend she was his. Even if it'd only been once, it *had* been.

When the talked turned to business, she proudly looked at Dan and affirmed him with her gaze. He was so smart and compassionate. Not at all the arrogant man she thought she'd found that first night.

"Who are your people, Dixie?" Jimmy asked.

She blinked, not having followed the change in topic. "I was a Jensen before I married."

"I knew some Jensens once," Jimmy said.

Uh-oh. Dixie maintained eye contact despite the urge to shrink behind the grandfather clock. When Dan moved a little closer and shot her a wink, her shoulder brushed his chest.

"My dad bought a couple of horses from a well-known trainer. Daddy said old man Jensen could communicate with the animals." Jimmy shook his head with a laugh.

Dan swirled the scotch in his glass. "We got a horse from him, too. I went to the Jensen's place with my dad when I was a little thing, maybe seven or eight."

Dixie's skin grew warmer, so she took her frozen margarita and pressed the cup against one of her cheeks then the other.

"The estate was amazing. Kinda gave me the vision for Southland. I remember thinking it was strange that old man Jensen seemed so much older than my dad and his kids were around my age."

"I hear you, man." Jimmy rocked back on his heels. "I think he had three children."

"His little red-haired daughter was riding my horse, a Chestnut Thoroughbred, around the track. I was scared to death to get on a horse that fast, but I wasn't about to let a girl outdo me." Dan winked as he sipped his drink.

"I heard he had a stroke that put him in bed, and he died many years later," Jimmy said. "He'd been a wealthy man, but the family had to sell everything off in the end, with him not able to work and the medical expenses piling up."

"That's the kind of care we hope to provide with our visiting nurses." Dan reverted into business mode once again.

Relief sagged Dixie's shoulders. She'd been ready for a new subject before the last one had begun.

"I wonder what happened to his kids," Dan said.

Oh no. Not again.

"I heard they've done well for themselves," Jimmy said. "Good breeding will do that for you. A dentist, an attorney, and I don't know what happened to the other one."

It was speak now or forever hold her peace.

Dixie straightened her spine. "She's a nurse." She allowed for a pregnant pause. "And she's standing right here."

***

Dan couldn't have been more shocked if Dixie had smacked him upside the head. He tried to save face.

"You never told me you were *that* Jensen family." He took her hand and held it.

"You never asked." She shrugged one shoulder and looked away.

There was the slap.

She was right. He was all set to commit to her *until death do us part,* but he hadn't taken the time to get to know her. It was no wonder she kept pushing him away at every turn.

Before they could discuss it further, dinner was announced. He held out his arm to escort her to the dining room.

She stared at it for a long moment and chewed the inside of her cheek. At the last second, when he was about to withdraw, she plastered a fake smile on her face and took his arm. He let out a slow breath.

Leaning close to her ear, he spoke softly. "Forgive me." He tried to convey his feelings with his eyes. "Stick with me a little longer, darlin'."

She ducked her chin, but not before he caught her grin. His chest thumped an unsteady rhythm when she leaned closer, pressing into his arm.

Dan picked at his food, and so did Dixie. His stomach tied itself into a tighter knot with every question Jimmy asked her about horses and her father, until he got around to the one they really wanted to know.

"Could he really talk to the animals?" Jimmy's eyebrows lifted expectantly.

She flattened her palms against the table and addressed their host. "Native Americans are very in touch with the life forces around them, and my daddy had the gift."

"Wow," Jimmy said. "I'm sorry to say this, but I never would've guessed you had Native American in the bloodline."

Me either. Especially since you had the chance to tell me. Now he knew for sure she could come up with something better than Clydesdale Dan. Sounded like the name of a porn star.

"I guess the Anglo genes dominated in the end. Daddy was part Hopi and lived with the tribe for a few years when he was young."

Dan's ears perked up. "My toast. The night we met."

She gave his thigh a light squeeze, and when she let go, he grabbed for her hand, twining their fingers.

"My brother, the dentist, got the dark coloring. My sister's blonde, and I'm..." She picked up a lock of hair. "Red."

"Did you get the touch?" Jimmy asked. "Can you talk to animals, too?"

Jimmy was half drunk, and Dan should intervene, but he wanted to know the answer so bad he could taste it.

"*That* is a rare gift," she said.

"*That*." Jimmy shook his finger at her. "Doesn't answer my question."

"Can I get another one of those margaritas?" Her eyes rolled back in her head. "So good."

"James," Martha called from the other end of the table. "Sweetheart, stop jawing and eat. We're ready for the next course down here, and you've barely touched your soup."

"We happen to be having a titillating conversation." Jimmy raised his glass to clink Dixie's fresh drink.

Dan's gaze locked with hers and titillating was

a word he would use to describe it. He was getting aroused in a way he needed to keep under control at the dinner table.

With people all around them, Francis tried to garner his attention. But he had eyes for only one woman.

When it was time to leave, Dixie stumbled a little, so Dan kept a tight arm around her. She slurred slightly, and it was apparent to him everyone thought she was friendly and socially elite, like the rest of them.

She hugged the necks of some of the women and kissed the cheeks of some of the men in farewell. Even though she was almost drunk off her butt, she staggered away as the most liked person at the party.

Dixie had a way about her, where your concerns became hers. She felt them deeply, and you knew you had an ally in her.

He helped her into the car then ran around to take the wheel. "Darlin', you are lit."

"I'm drunker than Cooter Brown." She giggled. "I like that you call me darlin'. If I weren't so drunk, I'd…" Her voice trailed off.

"What would you do, darlin'?" He put the car in gear and pulled onto the street.

"Nevermind. You're my boss."

"Can't you just forget about that while we're not at the office?"

She shook her head vigorously then froze, gripping the door handle in one hand and the console in the other. "I'm gonna throw up."

He pulled over. Porsche and puke did not go

well together. He went around and held her hair while she threw up.

Images from another life flashed through his mind, but he forced himself to remain in the present. "Please tell me you ate solid food tonight."

"I haven't eaten since breakfast on Monday, and it's all your fault. *'Come on a date with me to the senator's house.'*" She mocked him. "How am I supposed to eat with that kind of pressure?"

"Darlin', I didn't intend for you to be so worried about it. I'm sorry."

Dixie mumbled what sounded like the lyrics to a popular song based on her beverage choice for the evening. He pushed her back against the car seat and wiped her face with his handkerchief.

"Nice men carry handkerchiefs," she said. "My daddy told me that. He was old, but he was smart."

Dan went back to the driver's seat and took it slow and easy. "Why didn't you tell me about your family?"

She took a deep breath and turned her head away. "When your family goes from great to a shadow of greatness, you tend to downplay it a little bit."

"So you're embarrassed by your family?"

A quick rise and fall of her shoulders preceded her answer. "Yes and no. I'm proud of my dad's legacy, but I'm ashamed he lost it all."

"No one knows the future," he said. "We plan to take care of our families the best we can, but we can't predict what tragedy will strike next."

"Why are you lecturing me, Dan? I learned that lesson the hard way, with my father and with Steve.

I guess the universe is trying to tell me that no matter how good I have it, it can be snatched away at any time." She got quiet and covered her face with her hands.

He stopped again and reached across the console to put his arms around her. "Shh, darlin'. You're one of the strongest women I've ever met. You have three girls who I give you sole responsibility for raising right." He kissed the top of her head. "Whatever has happened to you, you've proven how brave you are because you're still here, standing tall."

"I'm sorry, but I have to vomit again." She opened the car door and leaned out.

For the remainder of the drive, she teetered on the edge of restless sleep. Once he got her home, he carried her in the house.

Maddie's lip quivered. "What's wrong with Mama?"

"Girls, I went to Margaritaville," she said with one last burst of energy.

Following Liz, Dan took Dixie to her bedroom and laid her on the bed, slipped off her shoes, and pulled the covers over her.

He kissed her cheek. "I don't care how drunk you get or how much you puke in my car. I love you, darlin'."

She pulled the blanket under her chin and made a noise in her throat. "I love you too, Big Dan."

When he checked on the girls, he found Katie consoling Maddie. He sat on the couch next to Liz and put his arm around her while Katie slid under his other arm and Maddie crawled onto his lap.

"Girls, your mama's fine. She just hadn't eaten any real food and had some alcohol. She was safe 'cause she was with me. You know I'll always take care of her and you girls too. You have my word."

Maddie looked at him with watery blue eyes. "Promise you won't take her to that village place again?"

He chuckled. "I promise, sugarfoot."

"Mr. Dan, does that mean you're gonna propose?" Katie asked.

"Katie, Mama would be so mad if she heard you say that," Liz said.

"Don't worry. I love your mama, and I love all of you. One day we'll be a family, but right now, your mama still needs some time." He paused, knowing he should end it there, but he couldn't resist. "You girls want in on my scheme?"

Liz raised a skeptical eyebrow while the younger girls squealed their affirmation. They both turned to their older sister.

Dan hoped he hadn't just made a huge mistake. "What about you, Lizabelle?"

The apples of her cheeks slowly lifted until her slightly overlapped front teeth showed behind her smile. "Mama could do worse."

Chapter Eighteen

Dixie had slept with her mouth open. It was the first thing she noticed when she woke up because she was pretty sure the cat had used her mouth as a litter box.

She opened her eyes and remembered they didn't have a cat.

Moaning, she turned her head to look at the clock. It was almost noon and all was quiet. The girls were probably eating Frosted Flakes in front of the television.

She sat up on the side of the bed and fought a wave of nausea. "I'm never drinking again."

Someone had left a glass of water and a bottle of aspirin on the nightstand. She forced a couple down and stumbled to the bathroom to find her toothbrush.

Upon seeing her reflection in the mirror, she let out a little scream. Her smeared makeup and ratted hair made her look like a creature from a horror movie. Make that a sleazy horror movie since she still wore last night's cocktail dress.

The events of the previous night all came flooding back to her.

Well, some if it came back.

She remembered meeting the senator and enjoying the margarita machine. After that, Dan must have carted her out of there when she'd started embarrassing him. There had been vomit on the side of the road, but the rest was a blur.

She was going to get fired for sure. There was no way the senator would sign the paperwork now. She might as well get her resignation letter ready and polish her résumé.

At least she hadn't dated Dr. Flint the Flirt. Maybe she could get her old job back at the hospital.

After taking a shower and putting on fresh clothes, Dixie felt almost as good as new, despite the dull ache in her head.

When she turned off her bathroom light, the smell of smoke hit her, and she called out to the girls as she sniffed the air, trying to track the source of the scent.

When they didn't answer, panic lodged in her throat.

Searching the kitchen, she found a note on the bar from Dan.

I took the girls to ride horses at Southland. Come join us when you feel better.

Dixie didn't know whether to be angry or grateful. Things were getting entirely too comfortable between her family and his. She needed to put the professionalism back into their relationship, but the truth was, as much as she tried, it had always been personal between them—*real* personal.

The typewriter was on one end of the dining table, her at-home office, so she sat and composed her resignation letter.

The trip to Southland was the longest of her life, and she wiped away tears as she turned into the driveway for what was probably the last time.

To her surprise, there were several cars parked out front. She stopped behind them and went around the side of the house to see Katie and four of her friends from school being led around the corral on horseback by the Baker men and Uncle Ben Hill.

"Mama." Maddie ran to her. "I rode the horse with Mr. Dan."

Dixie dropped to one knee and hugged her youngest. "What's going on here?"

"Katie's birthday party," Maddie said. "There's a cake and everything."

"Hey, Dixie," one of the moms called to her.

She walked over to greet them, trying not to act as bewildered as she felt. "Thank you for coming."

"Dan apologized for the last minute invitation," Cindy's mom said. "He's so thoughtful to take care of things until you could get here. He told us about your work deadline this morning."

"Thoughtful is one word you could use to describe him," Dixie said. *Manipulative and too eager to stretch the truth were others.*

"Handsome's another," Tiffany's mom said. "And richer than sin. You should go ahead and take him off the market before someone else does."

Dixie didn't care for the penetrating look Tiffany's mom was giving Dan's backside, as if she possessed x-ray vision.

"Hey, Mama." Liz joined them next to the fence. "Aunt May and I just finished decorating the cake."

"Thanks for helping her, baby."

"Did I hear someone say something about cake?" Dan asked.

Dixie's face burned as her temper ignited.

***

Curiosity pricked Dan's mind as Dixie folded a piece of paper and put it in her back pocket. He didn't know what it was, but from the tight lines around her eyes and mouth, he sensed it wasn't good.

"May I speak to you for a minute?" Dixie spoke through clenched teeth barely covered by a fake smile.

"I won't hear a word you say while I have cake on the brain. Come on, darlin'. Let's go sing *Happy Birthday* to our doll baby." He put his arm around her to usher her toward the house.

She pulled away and picked Maddie up, a move so subtle only Dan noticed the slight.

Once inside, he had to put up with more advances from Tiffany's mama, Cheryl, while she admired everything in the house, often adding the phrase, "That must've cost a fortune."

He turned to Dixie and rolled his eyes. When she suppressed a smile, he approached and put his hand on her waist.

Twisting her body to face him, she narrowed her eyes.

"Watch her," he said in a conspiratorial whisper. "She may cart off the silver if we turn our backs."

"Dan, why are you doing all of this?" Dixie's voice was low but firm.

"Our girl missed her birthday celebration last weekend, and I blame myself. I had to make it up to her."

"Do you hear yourself? She is *my* girl, not—"

"Un-uh-uh, we aren't going to argue over this. Get used to it, darlin'. She's *our* girl."

He walked away from her but not before her jaw set and her hand landed on her hip in the universal pissed-off-woman pose. No doubt, he would hear about this later.

After cake and presents, Dan, Dixie, and the kids walked their guests out to their cars.

"I'm gonna get Uncle Ben Hill to move your car around by the garage. You don't have to park out front like a visitor," Dan said to Dixie.

"I *am* a visitor."

"No, darlin'. You're finally home. You just won't admit it yet."

He spoke over her shoulder. "Girls, do you think we can get your mama on a horse?"

"Yeah, Mama, you've got to do it," Maddie encouraged.

"It's so much fun," Katie said.

"Did you ride too, Lizabelle?" Dixie put her arm around her oldest.

"I did. I kind of see what you mean when you

always say being on horseback is a place of power."

As they migrated toward the corral, Dixie asked him, "Have you always had eight horses?"

"I'm looking at acquiring the Roan and Bay. I need someone who knows something about 'em to help me make my decision."

Dixie ran her hand down the neck and side of the big animal. "You already know everything you need to."

"I want to know what you look like on this one," he said.

"I shouldn't. I need to help Miss May clean up and get the girls home."

The girls begged, and his boys joined in.

"Please, Mama D," Paul said.

Dan watched for her reaction to the nickname, but she didn't bat an eye.

Her mouth kept ticking on one side. "One short ride," she said, holding up a finger. "Then we've got to skedaddle."

"Dad, can we go down to the lake?" Danny asked.

He nodded at his son. "Sure. Let's get these girls ready. Little sugarfoot can ride with me again."

"I want my own horse." Maddie stomped one of her worn leather boots, kicking up dust.

Dixie raised her brows. "She's her mother's daughter. I was riding before I could walk."

Dan, Dixie, and the boys worked together to get the girls saddled and mounted.

Once Dixie slung her leg over the horse, her countenance changed. The tiny lines around her eyes faded as her entire body relaxed. In his mind,

Dan saw the little red-haired girl, flying like the wind with the same smile the woman before him now expressed.

As they headed down the path to the lake, Danny said, "I want to ride ahead."

"Wait a second, Danny." Dixie looked at Dan. "Will you fellas keep an eye on the girls?"

Dan studied her. "Yeah. Why?"

"I'm gonna race Danny to the lake." She clicked her tongue and nudged the horse.

Danny accepted the challenge and charged after her.

"Girls, that's a thing of beauty," Dan remarked.

"The horse?" Liz asked.

"No. Your mama in her element. Happy. At home."

***

With her head down, Dixie put all thoughts of the manipulative man she'd fallen for out of her mind and moved as one with the animal. In her body, endorphins, serotonin, and dopamine were releasing to give her a euphoric high. It always happened when she rode.

From the spring in his gait, she'd guess this horse was a natural jumper.

When she got to the lake, she slowed to speak to Danny. "Is there a creek?"

"Yes, ma'am. Down that way." He pointed to the west. "Why?"

"Follow and see." She was off again, racing alongside the water's edge until it waned and narrowed to a creek bed.

The spot she picked was wide enough so the

horse wouldn't be insulted and narrow enough that if her instincts were wrong, it wouldn't hurt too much.

"If you want to cross," Danny said, "it gets so small further down you can step across."

"This horse wants to jump something."

"How do you know?"

She shrugged. "I just do."

"What if you're wrong?" Danny's forehead etched with concern.

"If I'm wrong, then you get to watch me take a swim in shallow water."

He grinned.

She walked the horse deeper into the woods to get a little running room. "You ready, boy?"

The horse snorted, and it was the encouragement she needed. She nudged him and let him control the pace. The animal knew what he was doing.

Time stilled as they gracefully soared through the air, but the landing was a little more jarring than Dixie remembered from childhood.

"Awesome," Danny said. "You're really good with horses. Liz said you used to ride a lot when you were younger."

"My dad used us kids as guinea pigs after he trained a horse to be sure it was ready. Since I was the youngest and smallest, I got jockey duty more often than not."

"So you like going fast?" Danny's eyes widened in disbelief.

"Don't you?"

"Yes, ma'am."

Once she jumped back across, she and Danny trotted side by side to meet the others. He wanted to know all about her equine experience, and she wanted to know his.

By the time they saw the group ahead, she finally felt a connection with Dan's oldest son. His approval had been hard-earned and rewarding.

Her heart fluttered with a sense of belonging…and dread.

She should get out now before she was in too deep.

Chapter Nineteen

Back at the corral, Dan, with the help of Dixie and Uncle Ben Hill, hosed and rubbed down the horses while the kids went for a swim in the pool.

It was hard for Dan to stay focused on his task because his gaze kept drifting to Dixie in her fitted tee and well-worn jeans. With loose tendrils of auburn hair falling from her ponytail, she was windswept and beautiful.

"You looked right at home on that horse, Miss Dixie," Uncle Ben Hill said.

"Felt it too," she said with a smile of genuine pleasure.

"So do you think I should get him?" Dan asked.

"Do you or the boys jump? I think he can be developed to compete. He's that good. Of course, he likes to go flat out too, so I guess it depends on what you want him for."

He's a gift for my future wife, Dan almost said

out loud. After he shook himself, he asked, "What would you name a horse like that?"

"Oh, I never got to name the animals. They were always passing through and naming them kind of creates an attachment."

"But still, if you could pick a name, what would it be?"

"Depends on the horse."

"Stubborn woman, what would you name this horse?" He pointed to the animal.

"Testy," she said. "Someone must be getting low blood sugar. Do you need another slice of birthday cake?"

She was rarely sarcastic with him, but he liked it.

"Probably, but that still doesn't solve my problem."

"Sugarfoot," she said. "I always wanted a horse called Sugarfoot."

"That's what I call Maddie, and it's a sissy name for a horse," he said.

"Men can be so sexist, Sugarfoot." She kissed the horse's nose. "Don't let him get away with calling you a sissy."

The horse neighed.

"If I get kicked in the kneecap, it's on you, darlin'."

Back at the house, Dixie told her girls to get dried off, so they could go home.

"You can't go yet. Aunt May..." Dan called in reinforcements.

Aunt May came to the back door, wiping her hands on her apron. "Dem chirren is working up an appetite, I see."

"Dixie's trying to leave."

"Pfft. Tattletale," she grumbled.

"You can't do dat, Miss Dixie. Little Katie told me her favorite food's fried chicken, and I done been to the sto' and's frying it up now. We got biscuit in da oven, smashed taters, and field peas."

"Gosh, that sounds good," Dixie said. "But we've taken advantage of your hospitality enough already."

"Dem lies," Aunt May said. "No such thing with you and dem sweet gals."

The phone rang, and Dan excused himself to answer it.

"Mr. Baker, Trey Robertson. I have that information you wanted on Dixie Johnson."

"Just a minute." He stretched the telephone cord from the kitchen wall to the half-bath nearby and closed himself in. "What did you find?"

"First of all, I'm sorry it took me so long to get back to you, but I was hoping something would turn up. The worst thing I've got on her is she paid off her deceased husband's gambling debt to a bookie named—"

"I already knew that. The name's not important. What do her financials look like? Where does she spend her money?"

"She has a mortgage and a car loan, both through the People's Bank. Her checking account doesn't have much money left at the end of the month, but it all goes to living expenses and her daughters' extracurricular activities like Tonya's Dance School. Her savings account is healthy, and there are three joint savings accounts with her daughters' names on them. I'm thinking college funds."

"So, no red flags?"

"None, sir. I hope that doesn't disappoint you."

"It doesn't. Thanks, Trey."

Dan exited the bathroom to find Dixie and Aunt May giving him curious looks.

"What? I had to go." He hung the phone back in its cradle.

"Lawd-a-mercy. You ain't lived, Miss Dixie, 'til you taken care of four boys," Aunt May said.

"Can I speak to you in your office?" Dixie asked. "It's about work."

"Oh, yeah? I have something to tell you. You're going to Las Vegas as a representative of the company."

Her eyes widened. "What?"

"You heard me." He'd tugged the paper out of her back pocket when she'd been about to mount her horse.

He wouldn't accept her resignation. The fact she'd prepared one stung him a little.

"Why don't cha leave dem gals here with us while you go, Miss Dixie?" Aunt May asked.

"Oh, no. I could never do that," she said. "They can be a handful."

"They no worse than dem boys. I's take good care of 'em."

"I don't doubt that," she said. "But I have family I can ask."

"Well, if that don't pan out, you call Aunt May."

167

"I will, thank you."

Dan smiled because Dixie must've forgotten about the letter since she was thinking about childcare arrangements.

He would wait a little longer before telling her he was going to Vegas too.

***

Dixie followed Dan into his bedroom, and he closed the door.

She deliberately slowed her breathing to calm her excitement and try to get her scattered thoughts in order.

"Why are you being so nice to me?" she asked. "Are you in denial that I humiliated you in front of your friends last night?"

"You're a good actress. I really didn't know how shit-faced you were until I got you in the car. You were all over me."

"Liar."

He smirked. "Only about that last part. You handled yourself very well, darlin'. The others were much worse off than you. Martha and her sister got into a hair-pulling contest over a designer handbag."

"Un-uh."

"Uh-huh. You were charming and beautiful. Everything I'd dreamed, except for the vomit. That took it a little too far. Why didn't you tell me you hadn't been eating all week?"

Her eyes bulged. "Who told you that?"

"You did. And Lizabelle confirmed it. She was worried about you. Her maturity makes her worry about more things than she should."

Dixie turned her head away. "I was nervous

about the dinner party, and I lost my appetite."

He stepped closer, put his hand on her hip, and slowly skimmed it up her side. Her gaze followed, and she didn't move, though her body hummed like a tuning fork.

Don't let him notice.

His smirk told her he had.

"I think you could use a few more curves, but you're beautiful no matter what your frame looks like. There was no reason to get so stressed. They're people, just like you and me, but they're more screwed up. I need you to talk to me when you're feeling anxious or worried."

With his proximity, her brain turned to mush. His breath was warm on her cheek, and all she had to do was move a few inches to claim his lips.

"Dammit, Dan. I can't think straight when I'm around you." She tried to back away, but he gripped her waist with both hands.

"Why? What do I do to you?"

His bedroom eyes revealed he knew exactly what he was doing to her, and her heart kicked into high gear.

Just as he leaned in, there was a knock at the door. He turned her loose, and she pretended to look at some folders on his desk.

There was a scrap piece of paper that read: PI, Trey Robertson, DJ.

"Time to eat, D," Dan said. "We need to get some meat on those bones."

A chill ran across her skin, and she raised her head to sniff the air. "Is something burning?"

"That's probably fried chicken you smell."

She joined her girls and the Baker boys at the long dining table and wondered why it was so large. Dan's late wife must have entertained a lot.

As if they were sharing a brain, Maddie tugged Dan's shirtsleeve. "Mr. Dan, why do you have such a big table?"

"Ella said we'd need it someday, and I didn't question her. She kinda knew things sometimes."

"She's real nice," Maddie said.

Dixie froze with her fork halfway to her mouth.

"Yeah, she was a real sweetheart." Dan grinned. "She'd have to be to put up with me."

Dixie waited anxiously to see if Maddie would elaborate. Thankfully, her daughter's attention span had her moving on to the chicken leg in her hand.

After dinner, Dixie helped Aunt May clear the table, but May shooed her out of the kitchen, so she could wash the dishes.

"Girls, thank Mr. Dan, so we can get home."

They all begged to stay longer. The youngest Baker boys added to her girls' pleas, and Dan raised his eyebrows and the corners of his mouth in happy anticipation.

"I think we've more than taken advantage of their hospitality," Dixie said.

In response, she got groans, boos, hisses, and pouty lips.

"Before you go, I have one more present for you, doll baby." Dan gave Katie an envelope.

She tore into it and read aloud, "Certificate for one custom pageant dress designed by Clay Odom." Then she squealed her delight.

Dixie put her hand on her chest. "Dan, that's

too much."

"No, it's not, darlin'. She's gonna be the cutest doll baby in that pageant."

"Girls, get in the car." Dixie walked out without another word.

As she stomped toward her vehicle, she clenched her fist and screamed in frustration. That stubborn man would not take no for an answer.

Stopping midstride, she reached into her back pocket for her resignation letter only to find it wasn't there.

"Son of a—"

"Mama, are you okay?" Liz asked.

It must have fallen out of her pocket since her pants were a little loose.

She would just go home and type up another one. Then bring it back and nail it to his darn back door, the bullheaded jackass.

She slid behind the wheel and turned the key over, but nothing happened. The girls were still getting into the car when she tried again.

"Come on, you piece of crap." She pumped the accelerator.

"Mama, you said crap," Maddie pointed out.

"Don't repeat what I say." She patted the dashboard. "Come on, baby. You aren't paid for yet, so you have no right to let me down like this."

When the engine clicked and died, she laid her head on the steering wheel and sobbed.

"It's okay, Mama," Liz said. "Don't cry. Mr. Dan can help—"

"I don't want his help!" she yelled. "He helps too much."

Chapter Twenty

Dan had pushed Dixie too far. Part of him wanted to walk away and give her space, but he couldn't. She wasn't used to leaning on anyone, but she needed to get used to it and quick.

He opened the car door. "Pop the hood."

"Did you do something to my car so we couldn't leave?" Her glare could've melted an iceberg.

"I can't believe you'd ask me that." His bravado was fake because he had actually considered it.

He was guilty of other things, and when she found out, she'd be even more upset. But he wasn't going to let that happen.

"We'll see if we can jump it off." He raised the hood. "Danny, go get the truck and the cables."

Dixie stayed behind the wheel with her hands over her face, crying. It was all Dan could do not to take her in his arms. Instead, he took the jumper cables and hooked them to her battery.

"Try it now, D."

She turned the key, but nothing happened.

Just great. Dan shook his head.

None of his options seemed appealing. He could take them home in his Blazer or offer to let them stay. She'd probably accuse him of trying to get her into his bed while all their kids were in the house. He wasn't totally opposed to the idea, but he'd rather their next time be more private. But at this point, he was losing confidence there would be a next time.

"It's probably the starter," he told her. "Y'all take the Blazer home, and I'll see about your car tomorrow."

"No. No way," she said. "I'm never getting in that vehicle again."

"Now you're just being unreasonable. Take it and go. Or stay. Those are your choices." He busied himself putting up the jumper cables.

Dixie got out of the car and went into the house. The girls stayed put.

He leaned in the window. "I'll try to talk to her, but I think she's pretty angry with me."

"She's just upset about the smoke," Maddie said.

"What smoke?" he asked. "The car wasn't smoking, was it?"

"No, sir." Maddie twisted her lips but said no more.

Dan went in the back door to find Dixie on the phone. She hung up and closed her eyes. When the tear rolled down her cheek, he moved in and put his arms around her, no longer able to resist.

"I don't understand what's happening, Dan."

"Shh, darlin'. Try not to worry so much. Just relax and go with it. I mean, it's not life or death, is it?"

"I guess not." She sniffled. "I'm sorry I'm so cranky."

"It's all right every now and again. Just don't make it a habit."

She shook with laughter.

"Since you're staying, what do you think about camping out by the lake? We have enough tents for everyone. We can build a fire and roast marshmallows."

She opened her mouth then closed it, biting her lower lip. "That sounds nice actually."

Dan rounded up the kids and gave them all things to carry down to the lake. He handed Maddie a flashlight and told her to lead the way.

"She's too little," the older kids sang together. Laughter followed as they trudged down the path.

"I'm gonna load firewood on the back of the four-wheeler," he said to Dixie. "You can carry the marshmallows and ride with me."

The split logs were piled inside the woodshed, and Dixie helped him by picking several pieces of kindling from a five gallon bucket. "Why do you have weights on the front of the ATV?"

"It's light in the front end, so if I'm hauling anything, the weights keep it balanced."

"What do you haul?" She popped a marshmallow into her mouth.

God, he wanted to kiss her, but he kept

working. "Wood, kids, deer. You name it, I've probably hauled it."

"Why are you so great?"

He stopped to look at her. Those blue eyes were focused on him in what he hoped was admiration. Her full lips were slightly parted in anticipation of his answer.

"I want to be great in your eyes, Dixie." He set down the logs and stepped closer to her.

She slid her hand into his. "You already are. In fact, you're too good." Her gaze focused on where he twined their fingers. "I had it good once, and I lost it all. I'm not willing to go through that again."

"Darlin', you won't lose it all. And if you do, you're a strong woman. You'll land on your feet."

"How do you know?"

"Because you've done it before. You'll survive, and you'll do whatever you have to do to provide for your girls."

"You do too much for us." She looked down. "I can never repay you."

"I don't want you to repay me. I care about your girls, and I care about you. It's my pleasure to do things for all of you."

"You can't care so much, Dan. It's not…"

"Not what? Appropriate? Says who?"

"You're my boss."

"Okay. I'll fire you, if that's what you want."

***

Dixie thought she had been ready to resign moments earlier, but as soon as Dan suggested letting her go, fear surged through her. She turned away from him and took a few deep breaths to keep from hyperventilating.

His hands gripped her shoulders.

"I'm okay. I'll be okay. I could use a drink."

"After last night?" He put his palms out in front of him. "Sorry. Hair of the dog. Be right back." He walked the short distance to the detached garage behind the house.

While he was gone, she gave herself a pep talk.

He was right. She worried too much and apparently drank too much. Working for Dan relieved some of her stresses but created others. Her heart, her body, everything but her logical brain told her to take it to the next level.

Hold on to him and never let go.

Dan returned carrying a small red six-pack cooler with a removable white lid. "I hope beer's okay."

"You're right. I don't need it. I'm sorry again for the mini-breakdown." She took the cooler from him. "I'm not sure what's wrong with me, but I don't want you to fire me…and I don't really want to quit."

"But you can't stand being around me?"

"I actually like being with you, more than is appropriate for an employer/employee relationship."

"When we aren't at the office, why don't you just forget about that whole I'm your boss thing?"

"I wish I could. Life would be much easier if I could just enjoy your company without fear."

"What are you afraid of?"

"Everything. What people will say. If I'm crossing a line—"

"You crossed a line the night you met me. We both did, and I don't think either of us has been able to come back from it."

"It's all my fault. I'm sorry." She placed her palms on her forehead.

"Are you really?" The lilt in his voice lightened the mood.

"You're teasing me?"

"You bet I am. The kids are waiting. You want to hash this out later by the campfire?"

She smiled and let out a long breath. "There's nothing to hash out. Let's just have a little fun with our brood."

Down by the lake, Dan built the fire. The boys already had the tents set up, and Maddie bragged about holding the flashlight for them. Of course, there were electric lanterns too, but they let her take the credit.

Dan leaned over to Dixie's ear. "I put the cooler in my tent, in case you change your mind."

"Thanks." She suppressed a belch, which reminded her she'd overdone it the night before.

She didn't want to lose her chicken and biscuits, the first real meal she'd eaten all week.

"Mama, tell us a ghost story," Katie said.

Dixie only told ghost stories that weren't her own. If they were too real, they frightened her girls, and they knew enough to understand some things weren't made up.

Paul climbed onto her lap, so she stretched her legs out to accommodate him.

"Once upon a time, a little girl moved into a new house. Every evening her parents went for a walk, leaving her home alone. The first night, a few minutes after her parents left, there was a knock at the door.

"She opened it to a woman dressed all in black with long black hair, and her skin was white as a sheet. Her eyes were dark shadows.

"The woman spoke and her voice was like nails on a chalkboard, causing every hair on the little girl's body to stand up."

Dixie used her best witch voice. "'Do you want to see what I can do with my red, red lips and my long, long fingernails?'"

One of Paul's little hands gripped Dixie's knee, bunching up the loose fabric of her jeans in his fist.

Dixie smoothed a hand down his back before she continued. "The little girl's eyes widened as the woman held up her hand. The woman had the longest black fingernails she'd ever seen. The little girl was so scared she slammed the door and ran to hide in her room. The next night, the same thing happened. The woman said 'Do you want to see what I can do with my red, red lips and my long, long fingernails?' Again, the girl closed the door and hid until her parents came home.

"The same thing happened every night for a week until the girl was so upset that she hid when her parents left. One night, she gathered her courage and opened the door.

"'Do you want to see what I can do with my red, red lips and my long, long fingernails?'

"The little girl stomped her foot and answered, 'Yes, show me what you can do with your red, red lips and your long, long fingernails.'

"The woman put her fingers to her lips and went '*blll-blll-blll-blll-blll-blll.*'" Dixie strummed her fingers over her lips, making the noise.

Her girls joined her in making the sound, while Paul giggled and Johnny fell over on the ground laughing. Danny added to Johnny's laughter by tickling him.

The best reward for her storytelling was when Dan winked and nudged her, wearing a big grin on his handsome face.

Chapter Twenty-one

Heat radiated through Dan's chest. All around him, happy little details caught his attention. The younger girls were attempting to tickle Danny, and he was pretending it worked. Liz was teaching Johnny a rhyme, which included hand gestures, snaps, and claps. Paul snuggled against Dixie's shoulder while he made up a scary story to entertain her.

Dan didn't want the moment to ever end. He was enjoying his family and dreaming of their future.

"Hey, Dad." Danny stood with Maddie on his shoulders. "Can we roast marshmallows yet?"

Dan nodded. "Y'all go find some sticks."

The kids scampered off, and Dan slid closer to Dixie.

"What's it like really?" he asked.

"What?"

"The things you see."

The muscles around her eyes tensed before she turned her head away.

He rubbed her back with his palm. "I'm not making fun of you. Paul told me what he saw. I really want to know."

She shrugged. "It's usually like when you see something out of the corner of your eye but turn to find nothing there. Sometimes, there's something."

The kids returned more quickly than Dan expected. He shouldn't have underestimated the appeal of gooey sugar on a stick. His conversation with Dixie would have to be postponed until later.

When they'd roasted enough marshmallows to make little tummies sick, the children finally quieted.

Dan nudged Dixie. "Let's go for a walk. I have a surprise for you."

Hand in hand, he led her along the lakeshore. Turning to be sure they weren't followed, he opened his wallet and pulled out half a joint.

"What's that?" Dixie asked.

"Don't play innocent with me, Mama D." He lit it, inhaling deeply. Holding his breath, he passed it to her.

"Are you trying to make me see things, Big D?"

He shook his head as he exhaled. "No, darlin'. It helps with the nausea you're still experiencing from last night. Someone turned us on to it when Ella was sick from the chemo, and she didn't like to smoke alone. It calmed us both, so I kept a little of her stash."

"You must've been the best husband in the

world." She took the joint and sucked in a lung full of smoke before she coughed and a white cloud escaped her mouth.

"She always said I was, but I wish I could've done more." He kicked at a tree stump. "Have you seen her?"

Dixie inhaled again and held the smoke in her lungs for a long time before she blew it out. "Yeah, I've seen her."

She told him about the day in his office and the other times. He wished he could see Ella, but it was probably for the best he didn't. He'd wet himself and beg her not to come back.

"Do you think she wants us together?" he asked.

Dixie bit her upper lip. "I don't know. But we all have seasons in life. Maybe this is one of them."

"Daddy!" The screams came as the kids closed in. "The goatman is out there."

Dan pinched off the end of the joint and put it in his pocket. "What are y'all carrying on about?"

"The goatman," Johnny said.

The younger girls and boys wrapped themselves around Dan's waist, and he reveled in his role as protector. "You want me to shoot him?"

"I'll talk to him." Dixie walked in the direction they'd come from.

"No, Mama," her younger girls cried.

Danny and Liz looked on, laughing.

"I'll handle it," she said.

A moment later she returned.

"Mama, what did he say?" Maddie asked.

"He asked for directions to the high school. He

got lost and is supposed to be haunting the gym, not the woods at Southland. Don't worry. He won't be back."

Dan could tell she was trying not to laugh as she told her tall tale.

"Thanks, Mama D." Paul wrapped his arms around her waist.

She kissed the top of his head. "Anytime, cute stuff."

Dan smiled as he held her younger girls, one in each arm. Johnny stood with his back up against Dan.

"Danny Baker, Liz Johnson," Dan said, "I'll thank you to not scare the little ones again or else you'll be escorting them to the bathroom during the middle of the night."

"Yes, sir," they said in unison, covering their smiles.

Later, as Dan stoked the fire, he suggested they all sleep under the stars in their sleeping bags.

The night was pleasant, and it was the only way he would get to sleep beside Dixie.

***

In the pre-dawn hour, Dixie sat straight up, straining her ears to listen. The soft thud of boots against the earth slowed and halted, and she rubbed her eyes with her palms.

"Big Dan, Miss Dixie." Ben Hill was breathless.

"What is it?" Dixie popped up onto her knees, putting her arms in front of her to block the blow coming her way. "What's the matter?"

"I's so sorry, Miss Dixie, but yo house dun

burnt down." His voice was strangled with regret.

"What?" Dixie's voice was much louder than she intended as she got to her feet.

Dan stood beside her and put his arm around her as the kids began to stir.

"What's wrong, Mama?" Liz asked.

Dixie couldn't concentrate on anything other than the image of their house…gone. Her first thought was of the sentimental things she'd lost like her parents' wedding bands and the family photo albums.

A tug on her hand made her look down. Maddie stood there holding Spike the Horsey.

"Mama, don't be sad. I smelled the smoke, so we got some things from the house."

Dixie bent down to her. "Baby, did you have a premonition this would happen?"

She nodded. "Didn't you smell it too?"

Dixie wanted to yell at someone. What was the point in having premonitions if you couldn't do anything to change the outcome?

Anger gripped her soul, and she paced a few steps away so she wouldn't take it out on her daughter.

Glancing back, Dixie couldn't miss the alligator tears falling from her baby's eyes.

She dropped to one knee to be on level with Maddie. "I embraced it when I was your age, too. But it changed the day I knew my daddy was gonna die a long, slow, painful death, and there wasn't a thing I could do about it. Sometimes, I don't want to know the bad things that're coming."

"But, Mama," Liz said, "we got some stuff out

of the house. Something of Dad's we each wanted and the photo albums."

Dan spoke up. "I wondered why you girls packed suitcases to come out with me for the day. I thought y'all were bringing swimsuits and a change of clothes."

"Mama D." Paul tugged her shirt sleeve. "You can live here and sleep in my room if you need to."

Still on her knees, she turned to face him. "That's so sweet of you to offer, cute stuff, but there're too many of us. We'll find a place. Don't worry."

"You can have my room, too," Johnny said.

"Thank you, sweetie pie. Come here." Dixie hugged both of the younger boys. "The girls and I will be fine." *Maybe if she said it out loud, it would come true.* "Try not to worry, okay?" *Said the pot to the kettle.*

"Okay," they said in unison.

"Dixie, the girls can stay here while I take you to Bull Creek to see about the house," Dan said.

She blinked back tears. "Girls, I'm going to call Aunt Nancy and Uncle Larry and see about the house..." She sighed. "And the car..."

She had to hold herself together a little longer, so she envisioned putting on heavy armor. The imaginary protection might keep her from falling completely apart.

Liz hugged her. "You always say, 'when it rains it pours'."

Dan put his arms around both of them. "But every cloud has a silver lining, ladies."

"You guys are one big cliché." Danny patted

Dixie's shoulder. "What can I do to help?"

"Call the Harold's to come look at Dixie's car," Dan said. "I know it's Sunday, but tell Buford I'll make it worth his while. Liz, you help Aunt May keep an eye on the younger kids."

"Yes, sir."

As Dan guided Dixie to the four-wheeler, she was already making a list in her head of everything she'd have to replace. Having a task to keep her mind busy usually helped in moments of crisis, but this time, she had the overwhelming desire to join Ella Baker on the other side of this hard reality.

If Dixie didn't have three beautiful daughters who needed her, she might seriously consider checking out.

Chapter Twenty-two

Dan hid his amazement when Dixie got into the Blazer without blinking an eye. They hadn't been in the vehicle together since the night they'd met. Other things were obviously weighing heavier on her mind at the moment. He just hoped she wouldn't get more upset when she realized which truck she was in.

Right. More upset than losing your home. He shook his head.

He took her hand as he turned out of the driveway. "Darlin', we're gonna get through this."

"I know," she said. "My girls have been through so much. I don't understand why..." She covered her face with her hands and cried.

He pulled onto the grassy shoulder of the road, got out of the truck, and walked around to her side. After opening the door, he pulled her into his arms, where she bawled with her face pressed against his chest. Her body racked with sobs until she struggled for breath.

"Shh, darlin'. Calm down. You and the girls are safe." He smoothed her hair. "I know it hurts because you've lost so much. But you're gonna bounce back, and I'm here to help you in any way you'll let me."

She wouldn't allow him to do everything he wanted to do for her, so he would scheme, as quietly as possible, behind the scenes to see her and the girls taken care of.

He made a mental note to call the foreman and rush the construction of the cottage at Southland. It was intended for May and Ben Hill and almost complete, but they'd understand him offering it to Dixie.

They'd been living in an upstairs suite of the main house for a dozen years already. A little while longer wouldn't hurt.

He was proud of his younger boys for offering their rooms, but he knew Dixie would never consent to that arrangement. Living with a man outside of marriage was not something she would agree to. It was even more incentive for him to get her down the aisle.

"I'm sorry," she said between gasps for air.

"Don't be. You need to mourn what you've lost. Let it out. The house will still be waiting when you're ready."

A few minutes and a soiled handkerchief later, they parked on the street in front of the remnants of the Johnson home. A mask of solemnity slid over Dixie's face.

"Mrs. Johnson, I'm the Fire Marshall. I'm

afraid I have some bad news for you. It appears the fire was arson. Do you have any enemies?"

She clutched at her chest with one hand and took a step backward.

"She has no enemies." Dan introduced himself, explaining a little about Dixie's nursing career.

The police chief came over, and Dan did all of the talking because Dixie could only stutter and grasp her throat. He was concerned for her and wondered how to treat hysteria.

A little old lady shuffled toward them with a walking stick in one hand and a glass in the other. "Here, honey, have some sweet tea."

Dan took the glass and lifted it to Dixie's lips while she drank.

The woman addressed Dan. "The sugar will help with the shock."

"Are you a nurse?" he asked.

"No, but I taught school for forty years. I've seen children lose everything from houses to family members to family pets. I'm Marilee Whitmore." She extended her hand.

He shook it. "Thank you. She's taking this really hard."

Mrs. Whitmore put an arm around Dixie's waist. "The poor child has lost a lot in her life."

"It would be better if you didn't talk about me like I wasn't here," Dixie said.

"We're sorry, darlin'." He pulled her closer and kissed the top of her head. "We're just concerned."

"How are the girls?" Mrs. Whitmore asked.

When Dixie couldn't answer, Dan did. "Better

than you'd expect. They were ready."

"So, little Maddie had one if her premonitions again?"

"Yeah," Dan said. "Apparently so."

Another older lady approached. "I might have seen something, Dixie."

The police chief's head jerked up. "What did you say?"

***

Dixie was numb, as if she'd found a huge vat of topical anesthetic and dove right in. People were talking, but she didn't hear what they were saying. She stared at the charred remains of the house she'd shared with Steve and the girls.

She'd lived there since they'd married. He'd saved for a down payment while they dated, until Dixie finished her nursing degree. They'd only planned to have two kids. Maddie had been a surprise.

Dixie was unsure of when it had all fallen apart, but somewhere along the way, he'd stopped loving her and she'd stopped respecting him. The two things that were crucial for a marriage to survive.

He'd loved their girls though. The way he'd looked at Liz when she was an infant had revealed his heart. He'd been the same with all of the girls. But he'd never looked at Dixie with so much love in his eyes. She'd blamed herself for being a bad wife. She'd driven him to drink and the gambling had started because he didn't want to come home to her at night.

Dixie was sure she'd nagged too much and

been grateful too little.

Now, everything they'd once shared was ash.

Everything but their sweet babies.

Dixie blinked away tears, realizing she had so much to be thankful for.

After she'd answered all of the questions she could, Dixie hugged her neighbors then settled into the Blazer for the trip back to Southland. "You still have that weed?"

"Ah...yeah."

"Can you find a quiet place for us to stop and smoke it?" She had the urge to leave her body for a little while—to think about something, anything other than her current loss.

Dan turned into a field lined by woods on one side. She didn't even ask if he knew the owner. She'd learned Dan knew everybody. He valued his connections and sought to make them and reinforce them anytime he could.

He parked the Blazer in a wooded area, ripe with new growth.

She squinted her eyes as she peered out the window. "Is that marijuana growing over there?"

"Yep. The owner's my supplier."

Dixie didn't think twice before she climbed into the backseat.

Dan hesitated a moment, then followed. He fired up the joint, and she toked on it like a greedy addict. She missed the carefree days when she smoked a little to be able to handle her mother. Her father was never a problem. Of course, his limited speech kept him from complaining very much.

She laid it all out for Dan to hear—all of her

family's dirty laundry—and she'd been the wash girl. She hated them for it but loved them at the same time.

Dan listened and didn't say a word. When the roach clip held only singed paper, he hit it one last time then moved his mouth close to hers, shotgunning the last of the smoke.

She opened her mouth and took it, but if the truth were told, she wanted more. She wanted Dan…all of him.

Her lips remained close to his as she exhaled and claimed the kiss she so desperately needed.

He responded, and the next thing she knew, she was making out like a teenager in the backseat of the Blazer on a Sunday afternoon with the man her heart desired. She forced her eyes closed, not wanting to think or feel while they tugged at each other's clothes.

Dan growled at the sound of an engine approaching.

"This wasn't meant to be, was it?" she asked.

"Don't ever say that. From now on, we're only doing this at Southland, where I own the land. Deep in a remote area of the woods where the kids can't find us."

She grunted. "Good luck with that. I think our kids could find us blindfolded."

"All half-dozen of them. Hey…the Baker's half-dozen." He looked off into the distance. "I like it."

A truck stopped behind them, and Dan hopped out, tugging his shirt over his head. "Stay here."

Dixie kind of hated being told what to do, but

she loved feeling protected, which was what Dan was trying to do—safeguard her reputation.

She stayed low and straightened her clothes. If she could have one night alone with Dan, she would be a happy woman. She'd never complain again, even about losing her house. She'd just keep rolling with the hailstorms life kept unleashing on her, leaving her a little more battered each time.

The door opened and Dan climbed in. "I'm really sorry, but Guy thinks you're a hooker I picked up in Atlanta."

"Huh?"

"Stay down and don't ask." He cranked the truck and drove.

"A working girl, huh? Kinda true." She covered her face to laugh. Having slept with only two men in her entire life, the situation struck her as hilarious.

"I'm glad you think this is funny." He winked at her in the rearview mirror.

She leaned through the center opening and half hugged him with one arm. "Thank you for being so gallant. You keep this up, I might fall for you."

Once the words left her lips, she wanted to suck them back in.

Chapter Twenty-three

Dan's heart hammered in his chest as he parked the truck at Southland. He went around to open Dixie's door, and after helping her out, he laid one on her that Ajax wouldn't take off.

The sounds of yelling children drew his attention to the house, and he pulled himself out of lust brain, shaking his head.

Dixie beat him to the back door, and they walked into chaos.

Paul sat on the dining table, holding his arm, sobbing. Maddie was in tears, too, and the other kids were gathered around, talking loudly as Aunt May cared for Paul.

"What happened?" Dan asked.

"Paul and I were wrestling, and he fell down the stairs," Johnny said.

"What have I told you boys about horsing around near the stairs?"

"The playroom was crowded with all of us in

there," Liz said.

"It's broken, Dan," Dixie said, examining Paul while he screamed. "We need to take him to the hospital."

"Gwine, y'all. I'll watch the chirren." Aunt May turned to the kids. "No more horsin' around, ya hear? I'll get my switch after ya."

Dan handed the keys to Dixie and scooped Paul into his arms. He held his youngest son, who still whimpered, in his lap while Dixie drove them to the hospital.

Whatever calming effect the weed had delivered was long gone, and Dan's skin felt tight with anxiety. Since he had three rough-housing boys, he shouldn't have been surprised at a broken bone, but he hated to see anyone suffer, let alone his own child.

He sent up a plea to heaven in general and Ella in particular for Paul to be all right. His thoughts strayed to guardian angels and whether he really believed or not. When he glanced at the woman beside him, all doubt fled. Dixie was the answer to prayers he hadn't known he had.

At the Emergency Room, Dixie pulled some strings, and they were taken back fairly quickly.

Paul settled down once he was given medication for the pain, but he clung to his favorite nurse with his good arm. "Mama D, I'm glad you're here."

"I'm glad too, cutie." She kissed the top of his head.

Dan moved behind her and put his hands on her shoulders. "I like having you here, too. Thank you for standing by us through all the craziness." He planted a kiss on her cheek.

"Are you kidding?" she asked. "I'm pretty sure you held me upright in Bull Creek this morning. Otherwise, my legs would have crumpled beneath me."

"You don't give yourself enough credit, darlin'. It's been a hell of a day. But you know I'll always be here for you, don't you?"

She turned her head and squeezed his hands. "I'm going to go check to see how long we'll have to wait for x-rays." She patted Paul's leg. "Stay tough, little man."

***

Dixie found out what she needed to know and stopped to speak to several acquaintances along the way. While she was engaged in conversation, someone approached her from behind and covered her eyes.

"Guess who?"

She reached up and patted the hands, trying to place the voice. The heat from his body warmed her back—too close for her comfort. A sour taste filled her mouth as she inched forward putting more space between them.

"You're going to have to say something else." Dixie tried to wriggle out of his clutches.

He let her go and she turned.

"Dr. Flint…" Her mouth dropped open. "What are you doing down here?"

"I was in the unit and heard you were here. It's Ron now, remember?"

"Sorry, I forgot." She half-smiled as her cheeks

warmed.

"So, will I be seeing you in Las Vegas in a few weeks?"

"Yes…um…well, that was the plan, but things may have changed since my house burned down last night."

"Oh, Dixie, I'm so sorry. Was anyone hurt?" He moved his hands up and down her arms, checking her over.

She appreciated his concern for her wellbeing but could've done without the physical exam. "No. Thankfully, the girls and I were camping, but it was a total loss."

"Listen, I have a rental house. It's between the Creeks, and my renters just moved out. It's a little three-bedroom ranch. I need to have it cleaned, but you and the girls can move in pretty soon if you need a place."

To be sure her heart hadn't stopped from astonishment, she pressed her hand against her chest. "Oh, my God. Are you serious?"

Without thinking, she hugged him. "With the day I've had, I haven't even looked into a place for us. We can stay with my sister for a day or two, but that sounds perfect, Ron. Thank you."

"I'm glad to help out." His palms ran down her back, skimming over the top of her butt before he released her.

That same icky feeling she'd had when he'd been behind her returned, but she did her best to shake it off. The inappropriate touching was probably an accident. And even if it wasn't, she wouldn't ruin what seemed like a godsend by making something of it.

He escorted her back to the ER, and she stopped short of the room where Dan and Paul were waiting, not wanting Dan to see her with Dr. Flirt.

Dixie turned to face Ron. "I appreciate the rental. Let me know how much, and I'll drop a deposit or first month's rent check by tomorrow."

"Let me take you out to see the place first. We can negotiate a price then."

Dixie shivered at the ambiguity of his words and questioned whether renting from him was wise, but the offer was timely. She and her daughters were homeless.

"Also, if you can still make it to Sin City, I'll be glad to be your guide, show you around the place."

"Thank you, Ron. I need to get back, but I'll catch up with you tomorrow."

"You've got my number?"

She nodded and tried not to cringe as he leaned in and kissed her cheek.

Turning away, she caught Dan watching her from the doorway, looking none too pleased.

***

Dan's blood began to boil at seeing Dixie with Dr. Ron Flint.

She approached the door of the room, but he stood his ground, arms crossed, blocking her entry. "Who was that?"

"Dr. Flirt, I mean Flint. He's one of the ICU docs. I ran into him down the hall. Turns out he has a vacant rental house. It's big enough for the girls and me until we can rebuild."

Dan's ire rose even higher. The doctor not only wanted Dixie for himself, he wanted to provide a home for her and the girls, to be their knight in shining armor. Dan wasn't having it. He'd call every builder in the area if he had to.

"I'm not sure that's a good idea," he said.

"Do you have another solution to my current lack of living quarters?"

His solution was for her to marry him and move to Southland with the girls, but he knew better than to suggest it at the moment.

"I know people. I'll ask around," he said. "Maybe I can get you a better price. Hell, if nothing else, I'll put a mobile home at Southland, and y'all can stay there."

She touched his arm. "That's sweet, Dan, but you've helped me so much already. This place kind of fell into my lap, and I don't believe in coincidences. Everything happens for a reason."

"Agreed." He planned to give her reasons to be with him at Southland, not Dr. Flirt, as she called him. "That's why you were camping in my woods last night, instead of trying to get your girls safely out of a burning house."

When she flinched, he immediately regretted his harsh words and reached out to pull her close.

"I'm sorry, darlin'. I didn't mean to put that image in your head. I'm glad you're all safe. I'm sorry I'm an ass and say insensitive things sometimes." He was borrowing a word from Lizabelle.

Dixie leaned into him. "That image was already in my head. If my car hadn't conked out and

I hadn't been angry with you and refused to ride in the Blazer, I could have put my girls in danger." She looked up, her eyes filling with tears. "Who would want to hurt my family?"

"I don't know, darlin', but I'll do everything I can to keep you safe."

"Mama D," Paul called from the room.

Dixie let go of Dan and wiped her eyes as she moved to Paul's side. "What is it, cutie pie?"

Heat spread through Dan's chest as Dixie answered to the name his youngest son had been calling her since the day she'd saved his life. Once again, she was his son's heroine, and Dan felt the desire to have her, to be close to her. But then, that desire had been with him every day since the first night he'd met her.

"Will you stay with me if I have to spend the night?" Paul asked her.

"I would love to stay with you, but usually with a broken arm, you'll get a cast and sleep in your own bed tonight."

"Will you stay with me there? The girls can have my bed, and I'll sleep on the floor with you."

"Buddy," Dan said, "we can't ask Miss Dixie to sleep on the floor. You two can have my bed. I'll take the couch."

"Dan," she said, "I can't. I…don't even have clothes to wear to work tomorrow." She wiped a stray tear.

Most men detested a crying woman, but Dan loved having her lean on him. He hated that she was hurting, but he wanted to be her shoulder to cry on.

He needed to find a payphone and call Nora

Cook. She could help with clothes for Dixie and the girls. And he could call some other folks about rental properties. A mobile home would take a few days to get set up, and Dixie would kick up a fuss if he tried it.

"Look, darlin'. We're running out of daylight. Stay at Southland tonight and we'll figure out the rest tomorrow. Hopefully, we won't have any more injured kids when we get home."

Chapter Twenty-four

Dixie felt like an intruder lying in Dan's bed with Paul cuddled up next to her. Somehow, Dan had convinced her to stay, but the idea of sleeping in his and Ella's bed made her uneasy.

It wasn't just from seeing Ella hovering around Paul. She'd seen that since she'd walked in the door at Southland and found him injured. It was knowing the love they'd made in this bed, in the house they'd built together. Dixie wasn't sure she or Dan would ever be free of Ella's ghost.

Dan had been serious about their next romp in the backseat of the Blazer being at Southland. But she hadn't wanted to go there for fear of an audience with his deceased wife. If she kept her eyes closed and her mind focused only on him, she might be able to get through it. Otherwise, exhibitionism was not her thing.

"Let me know if y'all need anything," Dan said before he left the bedroom for the couch.

He could have easily slept upstairs with one of the boys since the girls took Paul's room, but he'd insisted on being nearby on the first floor, in case they needed him.

Generally, it rubbed her the wrong way, but she was learning to love that Dan Baker wasn't a man who took no for an answer. He was a man who knew what he wanted and went after it with all his might, reminding her of her father.

Her dad had been stubborn too when he'd refused to give up and die. The thought flooded her with guilt. Her dad had strained every day to hold on a little longer. In the end, it had broken their family.

Sometimes, men thought they had all the answers. They pushed the people they loved too far. Dixie saw her father's determination in Dan, and it scared her to death. At this point in her life, she couldn't handle more loss, but her heart was already lost to Dan Baker.

Tomorrow, she'd find her own place and start sending out résumés. It was a bad idea to fall for your boss and an even worse idea to pretend you didn't feel anything. If she didn't work for him, maybe they could date. Maybe Dr. Flirt could help her get her old job back.

Unease crawled down her spine as she considered the price she might have to pay for that.

A full bladder woke her during the night, and she stumbled in the dark toward the master bathroom. She tripped over something and began a slow motion descent as gravity combined with inertia sent her sprawling.

Strong arms enveloped her as she landed, and all of the air in her lungs escaped on impact.

Dan groaned as he took the brunt of her weight, not to mention her knees and elbows. "Damn, darlin', you may have just rendered me impotent." One of his hands moved between his legs.

"I'm so sorry. What are you doing on the floor?"

"Besides catching you when you fall? I couldn't get comfy on the couch."

Dixie rolled off of him and stood next to the pallet he'd made from quilts. "Why didn't you just get in the bed?"

"I didn't think you'd be too happy if you woke up and found me there. Was I wrong?" He knew her well.

"I've gotta pee." She went into the bathroom and closed the door.

Maybe she should do something out of character—shake things up a little. The problem with that was she'd been shaken enough in the last year, heck, in the last twenty-four hours.

She dreamed of security and stability, but they were as elusive as the pot of gold at the end of the Irish rainbow.

She returned to the bedroom to find Dan in the bed on the other side of Paul. He'd turned on a small desk lamp, so she could get back to bed safely. She crawled under the covers and rested on her side, facing Dan and his son.

He propped himself up on one elbow and whispered over Paul's sleeping form, "Do you want me to go?"

"No." She rolled onto her back and suppressed a smile. "Good night."

***

A ringing telephone woke Dan, and he sat upright in bed, rubbing his eyes. He blinked to focus and take in the sight, which made the corners of his mouth turn up.

The king-sized bed was over maximum capacity.

At some point during the night, all of the kids had found their way into his bed to join him, Dixie, and Paul. They were a tangle of arms and legs sprawled in every direction.

Aunt May knocked on the open bedroom door. "I declare, Big Dan, you gone have to get a bigger bed if all dem chirren gone sleep in it."

"Tell me about it. Who's on the phone?"

"Mr. Harold. They done got Miss Dixie's car fixed up but can't run it out here 'til later. Said she can come get it if she needs it sooner."

Dixie sat up in the bed too. "I guess I need to get it, so I can start putting my life back together. Can you give me a lift?"

Dan reached over and squeezed her hand. "Gladly. We better get these kids moving, so they can get to school."

A chorus of groans filled the air. "Dad, it's the last week of school. Let us skip today," Danny said.

"I can't," Liz said. "It's final exams, but…oh, crap. All of my school books are ash. Shit."

"Lizabelle!" Dixie squeaked.

"Sorry, Mama. I meant *shoot*. Do I have to put soap in my mouth?" Lizabelle's face had the most pitiful expression on it.

Dan laughed. "I think the teachers will understand and give you girls a reprieve. Paul gets to lay out because of his arm, but Danny, Johnny, move your asses."

"Language, Dan, or I'll get a bar of soap for you too," Dixie said.

He crossed his eyes, causing the girls to giggle. "Yes, ma'am."

"Girls, we need to go clothes shopping," Dixie said. "Get your things while I call the school."

Dan cleared his throat. "I called Nora last night. Go by Cookie's Closet, and she'll fix you up."

Dixie chuckled. "Ha-ha. I can't afford to shop there. We have to go to Turtles, Girdles, and YoYos."

"Maa-maa," Liz dragged the word out.

"Lizabelle's embarrassed to wear clothes from the T,G, & Y," Katie said.

"There's nothing wrong with clothes from there," Dan said. "However, I have a store credit at Cookie's that'll never get used since I don't wear ladies' clothes."

The girls giggled again and shifted around on the end of the bed.

"How did you get a store credit if you don't wear ladies' clothes?" Dixie asked.

Dan glanced down at his hands in his lap. "Ella did a lot of business there."

It was a true statement, and he hoped just ambiguous enough to satisfy Dixie and play on her sympathy.

She placed her hand on his arm. "I'm sorry."

"Don't be. Just do me a favor and use the credit." She'd never have to know Nora had instructions to put it on his account and send him the bill.

Chapter Twenty-five

Dixie got suspicious when Nora kept insisting the store credit was much higher than the amount of what they'd already picked out. The girls each had two outfits, and Dixie had chosen one from the sale rack for herself. The calculations she'd done in her head approached the three hundred dollar mark.

Dixie finally told the girls they had enough. The next stop was the dollar store for underwear, socks, and shoes.

Since Dan said he was going into the office for a few hours, Dixie used a payphone to check in. He'd given her strict instructions to take the day off and take care of her personal business.

"Dixie, I'm so glad you called," Betty Jo said. "Your sister needs you to call her. People have been dropping bags of clothes by her office for your girls."

The lump in Dixie's throat prevented her from speaking as liquid flowed from her eyes and nose.

When had she turned into an emotional wreck? She was tougher than this, but so touched by the kindness of others.

She pulled one of Dan's handkerchiefs out of her pocket and finally managed to respond. "Okay. Thank you."

"Dixie, my daughter's about your size, and she recently cleaned out her closet. She wants to offer you her clothes. Wait a minute, the Big Boss is about to take the—"

"Are you okay? Do you need me?" His deep voice wrapped around her like a blanket.

"We're fine."

"Good. Aunt May's expecting y'all for dinner."

"I can't. I'm taking the girls to Nancy's, so I can meet Dr. Flint and see the house."

The only sound on the line was of teeth grinding.

"Careful, you might break a tooth and have to pay my brother a visit," Dixie said. "Don't be angry. You know I have to do this."

"I know, I just wish you'd let—"

"On my own, Dan. I can take care of my family. I'm a big girl, been doing it for years."

More grinding noises. "Will I see you tomorrow?"

"I'll be in as soon as I take the girls to school. I'm not gonna make 'em ride the bus since it's the last week, and we don't know where we'll spend each night."

"If you'd just stay at Southland, you'd know."

"Can Betty Jo hear you right now? Don't do this to me. I'm your employee—"

"Relax. She stepped out for a smoke." He sounded like he was talking through clenched teeth. "I think I'll go join her."

Click.

She pulled the phone away and looked at it before returning it to her ear. "Dan?"

A dial tone answered her.

She put the receiver down and fought a wave of emotion. He was angry with her, but she needed to stand her ground.

The realization that she was too late reminded her of the resignation letter she'd lost.

She was in between a rock and a hard place. She needed the security of her job, but she also needed Dan.

No wonder her dad had always said don't crap where you eat. She would have to choose, and at the moment, she needed the job more.

That evening, Dixie parked at the hospital and got out of her car.

"Thanks for meeting me, Ron. I have my checkbook, so if everything works out, I can give you a deposit tonight."

"Calm down, Dixie. We'll get to the business stuff later. Have you eaten?"

Dixie didn't want to eat. She wanted to see the house. "No."

"Good. I'm starved. Hop in and we'll swing by the diner for a quick bite then head to the rental."

"I can just follow in my car." She bit back her frustration.

"Nonsense. Get in." He opened his passenger door.

An inner battle raged. She didn't want him to get the wrong idea. Then again, he was only offering a meal and a house to rent. Maybe she was the one with the wrong idea.

What could it hurt? Dr. Flint had always been nice, even if he did go through women faster than a knife fight in a phone booth.

Holding onto the door frame, she sank lower and lower until her rump met the leather of the Corvette seat. She was glad she was wearing pants because a skirt would have ridden up to the Promised Land.

A little later, Dixie laughed over pancakes and bacon as Ron regaled her with stories of his previous conference trips. He'd talked her into having breakfast for dinner, and it was a good choice. It reminded her of how her dad had often requested the same when she was young.

She forced her thoughts back to the present conversation. The more she heard the more excited she got about the trip. She hoped she'd have everything settled by then.

"Tell me about Las Vegas," she said.

"You're going to have a ball. I'll take you to see some shows. There are all sorts of entertainers, singers, showgirls, gambling…"

His enthusiasm was contagious, even though none of the things he mentioned really interested her.

***

The next morning, Dan beat Dixie to the office, and when her car pulled into the parking lot, he waited by her office door with his arms crossed over his chest.

All he could see in his mind was Dr. Flirt with his lips on a cheek that didn't belong to him.

Dan's foul mood faded as soon as she rounded the corner and beamed at him.

"We have a place." She practically skipped. "I would ask you to help us move in, but we don't have anything to move." She laughed.

His heart warmed at seeing her so happy. He hadn't seen it enough since he'd met her.

"From what I hear, you need a truck to haul all the clothes you've gotten," he said.

"Isn't it amazing? I'm overwhelmed at everyone's kindness."

Dan bit his tongue to keep from saying, "Everyone but me."

Instead, he said, "I'm glad for you. You know where to find me if you need me." He returned to his office and closed the door.

Sitting in his chair, he swiveled to look out the window. There was no way he could concentrate on work. The sky was bright blue and cloudless.

He stood, needing to escape the melancholy that had overtaken him as soon as he'd dropped Dixie at her car the previous day. He hated it when a plan didn't come together. The thought triggered the theme song from the *A-Team* to play in his head.

On a whim, he snatched his keys of the desk and drove straight home. In the garage, he took the cover off of his Harley. The rumble of the engine instantly improved his outlook. Once the wind plastered his hair back, he was almost a new man.

He burned up every back road in five counties

and returned home after dark. The boys had already eaten, and Aunt May heated him a plate in the microwave.

"Miss Dixie called," Aunt May said. "Wanted to take you up on your offer."

"What offer?"

"She had so many clothes to haul to the new house she thought she'd have to make several trips. Said you offered your truck and that sounded right to me. I sent Ben Hill to help her."

"Thanks, Aunt May." Dan attacked the meatloaf like a starving man.

He'd made a decision on his ride. Dixie had been right to want to keep their relationship professional, and he would work hard to get back there. Even though he loved her and her girls, it was evident she didn't return the sentiment.

He wanted a woman who looked at him like Ella had, with love and respect. He smiled at the memory of his wife's eyes. Sometimes, when he thought her face was beginning to fade from his mind, he'd pull out the photo albums.

That night, after he tucked the boys into bed, he did exactly that.

He dozed off sitting in the middle of their king-sized bed, surrounded by images of the good life. The one he missed. The one he wanted to have again.

Chapter Twenty-six

By the end of the next day, Dixie realized she'd done something wrong. Dan was distant, and his smile didn't meet his eyes. When she'd consulted with him on their project, he'd stopped getting personal, except to ask about the girls.

She should've been relieved he was being professional, which was what she'd wanted from the start. But now that he was, she knew what she was missing.

She wanted to be called darlin' and to have someone to share her life with.

Dan had already left work, and Dixie was about to go pick up the girls on their last day of school. As she approached the front desk, a man stood there in conversation with Betty Jo.

"Yes, but I really should deliver this report to Mr. Baker myself," he said. "I meant to be here earlier in the week, but something came up."

"Hey, Dixie," Betty Jo said when she saw her.

"Are you going to see Dan later? Can you take this to him?"

The man pulled the manila folder from the desk and held it to his chest. "I'm afraid I can't allow that."

"I'm Dixie." She extended her hand to the man and gave him a friendly smile. "And you are?"

"Trey Robertson. It's nice to meet you, Miss Johnson."

Dixie cocked her head to the side. She hadn't given him her last name, but his did ring a bell. Maybe they'd met before.

"If you'd like, Mr. Robertson, I can escort you to Dan's office. You can place your report on his desk, and we'll lock the door as we leave." Dixie tried to be helpful.

He stared at his feet as he shuffled them. "I guess that would be all right."

Dixie led the way down the hall to Dan's office and waited outside while Trey Robertson put the folder on the desk.

On the way out, he turned the lock on the inside knob before shutting the door behind him. Then Dixie led him to the reception area.

"All right," she said. "Have a good weekend, Betty Jo. I'll see you Monday."

"Wait, Dixie, your sister's on the phone for you. She says it's urgent." Betty Jo held out the receiver. "Goodbye, Mr. Robertson."

Dixie waited until he was gone before she put the phone to her ear. "Hello?"

Betty Jo reached for it. "No one's on the line. I needed to talk to you. Aren't you dying to know what that was all about?"

"Sure. But it's none of our business."

"Pah-lease. Dan would pick that lock faster than you could say 'jack-rabbit quick' to see what it was about."

"No. He's too honest. He wouldn't do that."

"Trust me. You've been looking at him through rose-colored glasses, but I've been working for him over ten years. He's a man who gets what he wants by any means." Betty Jo stepped around the desk with a key in her hand and walked down the hall.

Dixie followed, intending to talk sense into Betty Jo. "We should let his personal business stay that way. It's not right for us to pry."

Betty Jo had the door open and the folder in her hands before Dixie could make any more objections.

"You might want to see this." Betty Jo held out the folder.

Dixie took it and thumbed through the pages—her bank statements, employment history, income tax forms. "What? Why?"

"What in the hell are you ladies doing in my office?"

***

Dan nearly laughed at the stunned expression on Dixie's face and the guilty one on Betty Jo's.

Dixie dropped the folder she held and papers scattered. He bent to pick them up but froze when he saw what it was.

He left the mess on the floor and stood slowly. "I can explain."

"Why you hired a private investigator to spy on

me? Save your breath. Consider this my two weeks' notice."

"Your employment contract requires four weeks and written notification. If you have questions about it, you can take it up with your sister. She drafted the contract for me."

"You son of a bitch—"

"Hey." He put a hand up. "I didn't invite you into my office to look into my private documents. I suppose I could fire you over that. Betty Jo, too. But I don't want to lose either of you. If you'd calm down and let me explain—"

"Hear him out, Dixie," Betty Jo said. "Even though he's a sneaky bastard, he almost always has good intentions."

"After that day at the racetrack," he said. "I needed to know if you were into anything shady or dangerous."

"You sent a PI to talk to the bookie?"

"He knew about it, but I didn't tell him. I assume he followed some other lead."

Dixie gasped as her hand covered her mouth. She moved past him and out of the door.

He grabbed her arm. "What is it?"

She looked at where his hand gripped her arm, and he let go. He hadn't meant to grasp her so hard.

"I want to thank you, Mr. Baker," Dixie said. "You could have asked me anything you wanted to know, and I would have told you. I'm not a liar like you. Thanks to your PI and his snooping, I have a good idea who burned my house down." She disappeared around the corner.

"I'm the biggest ass in the whole world," he

said.

"Yep." Betty Jo slapped him on the back. "But you're our ass, and we love you. You couldn't have foreseen the consequences."

"Yeah, but she and the girls still might be in danger. Get the sheriff on the phone."

***

Dixie cried all the way home. She wasn't sure if she was angrier with Dan for what his meddling had caused or herself for misjudging him so badly.

The inside of the car turned frosty.

"Go away," she screamed in frustration. "I don't want your stupid husband."

The temperature normalized, and Dixie dried her eyes as she pulled into the driveway of the rental house. It was then she realized she'd forgotten to pick up the girls from school.

She laid rubber back to town.

Half an hour after the final bell had rung, the school was like a ghost town. Tumbleweeds of crumpled paper rolled across the parking lot where only a handful of cars remained. Normally, the girls waited out front if she was late, but she didn't see them anywhere.

Dixie parked the car and ran inside. The secretary in the main office said the girls had been outside when she'd last seen them.

Dixie's heart raced, and heat spread up her neck as the pounding in her head increased. She needed to stay calm and think about where they might be.

Borrowing the phone, she called her sister at work, but Nancy hadn't seen the girls.

When Dixie explained about the PI and the bookie and the possible link to the house fire, Nancy said she was calling the police.

Dixie didn't know where to go, but she had to find her daughters. First, she drove to Nancy's house, hoping Sheila might know where they were, but no one was home.

She let herself in and called Nancy again. "Where's Sheila?"

"She went home with a friend. Where are you? The police went to the school, but you weren't there. Dan's looking for you, too."

"Why'd you call him?"

"He called me after he called the sheriff about the bookie. I wish you would've told me. You could have asked me for help, but you let your pride get you into this mess."

"You're right, Sister. It's all my fault that my kids may have been kidnapped and killed." Dixie slammed the phone down.

Sucking in a few shallow breaths, she wished she would have taken the time to call Ma Bell about hooking up the telephone in her new temporary house.

She knew she should go to the police station, but she wanted to try home one more time. It struck her that Ella's earlier appearance might have been about her girls and not Dan at all.

"I'm sorry. Ella, I'm sorry." She cried so hard she made herself sick, unfit to drive even, but she drove anyway. She wouldn't stop until she found her girls.

When she pulled up to the rental house, Dan's

truck was in her driveway. She shouldn't be surprised at him being all up in her business...again.

Her fear and frustration faded when the door opened and the girls came out. She'd never known such relief until that moment—relief that was quickly replaced with indignation.

Her tirade would have to wait though because a sheriff's car turned in behind her.

***

Dan clenched his hands into fists to keep from reaching out for Dixie as she approached. Her face was red and splotchy. Lines of mascara streaked her cheeks, and she pinched the bridge of her nose.

He'd gotten to the house moments before to find the girls inside. When Dixie was late picking them up from school, their cousin Sheila and her friend had offered to take them home.

Lizabelle had said she intended to call someone to let them know, but she'd forgotten the phone hadn't been connected yet. They'd been there when Dixie came home the first time, but she never got out of the car.

He blamed himself for upsetting her so much she forgot the girls at school.

"Bob." Dan extended his hand to the deputy sheriff. "How are Nora and the boys?"

"Good, Big Dan. Thanks for asking. You and your boys?" The deputy raised his eyebrows.

"Gettin' along. It's these little ladies we need to be worried about." He gestured to Dixie and her daughters.

After going inside, Dixie sent the girls to their

rooms before explaining her suspicions to Bob Cook.

"Miss Johnson, do you have a safe place you and your daughters can spend a few days until we have time to investigate?"

With her thumbs pressed against her brow bones, she answered, "This place was supposed to be safe. I don't want to put anyone else in danger."

"Come stay at Southland," Dan said. "The cottage is supposed to be finished today. You and the girls can stay there for a little while."

"That's May and Ben Hill's place. We can't push them out."

"They've been in the upstairs guest suite for so long, it'll take them a while to get packed and moved. I promise they won't mind. They'll want you and the girls to be safe. Bob, can y'all put a deputy on the road at night until I can get a gate installed?"

"Not a problem," the deputy said. "It's settled then. Miss Johnson, I'll contact you at Big Dan's number to let you know what we discover."

When the sheriff left, Lizabelle came into the living room with a pill bottle and a glass of water. "Here you go, Mama. I'll get your sunglasses."

Dixie's hand covered her eyes as the younger girls closed the curtains to block the late afternoon sunlight.

Dan watched in silence for a moment then asked, "What's going on?"

"Ingrain," Maddie said.

"No, it's a migraine, Sister," Katie corrected as she tried to crack open a metal ice tray from the freezer. "Mr. Dan, can you open this? I need to make an ice pack for Mama's head."

Dan helped the girls take care of their mama who'd started vomiting. "This is twice you've blown chunks on me, D. I'm starting to think you don't like me."

"Sorry." She spit into the mixing bowl she'd just yacked in.

"Mama, do you need to go to the ER for a shot of Phenergan?" Liz asked.

"I don't know." Dixie groaned as tears streamed from beneath the sunglasses.

"Girls, go pack a few clothes…hell, pack everything you can in the back of my truck and your mama's car. I'll take y'all to Southland and then your mama to the hospital if she's not better."

"How are we gonna take two cars?" Liz asked.

"You're gonna drive one of 'em, sweetheart." He smiled as Lizabelle's face lit up.

Dan didn't see the harm in letting a mature twelve-year-old, whom he'd seen drive go-carts, maneuver the back roads in his truck. He'd been driving by that age; of course, on the farm it was mostly tractors.

He took Dixie and the girls in Dixie's car and Liz followed in his truck.

Since Dixie dry heaved most of the way to Southland, he decided she needed medical assistance. After all, the first thing she'd lost had been the medicine meant to quiet the migraine.

"Good job, Liz." He complimented her driving ability as the girls grabbed some of their things out of the two vehicles. "I need you to help Aunt May take care of the girls and boys. Call your Aunt Nancy to let her know where you are."

Dixie laid across the front seat of her car with her head in his lap as he drove to the ER.

Trying to hold the ice pack in place with one hand as he steered with the other, he had flashbacks of when chemo and radiation treatments had debilitated Ella.

He carried Dixie into the hospital then name dropped like a champ to get her straight back to triage.

A couple of shots later, he pushed the wheelchair to the car and met Nancy in the parking lot.

"Oh, my God, Sister. I know you hate me. I'm sorry for what I said." Her voice was full of remorse. "I'm sorry you're so sick, sweetie. What can I do?"

Dixie, still wearing her sunglasses, shrugged.

"Follow us back out to Southland," Dan said. "You can help her get settled."

"I'll be right behind you. I'll call Dr. Flint to cancel your date."

"What date?" Dan's spine stiffened.

Chapter Twenty-seven

Dixie was in a cycle of waking and sleeping. She needed to get up but was so groggy she couldn't manage. When her bladder wouldn't allow her to stay in bed any longer, she sat up and tried to move her heavy limbs.

The inside of her eyelids were lined with a hundred twenty grit sandpaper. When she managed to keep them open long enough to take in her surroundings, she realized she was in Dan's bed, again.

She closed her eyes and almost fell asleep sitting on the side of the mattress.

"Do you need some help, darlin'?"

She loved his voice. It vibrated her eardrums and sent tiny shockwaves straight to her heart…and beyond.

The weight of her cheeks prevented her from smiling, so she nodded in response. The movement was difficult to control, and she almost fell forward.

"I've gotcha." Strong arms lifted her. "We need to get some fluids in you as soon as you can manage."

Her forehead rested on his chest as he stood her in front of the toilet.

He held her by her upper arms until she was able to hold her head up and look at him.

"I'm not leaving you by yourself. Pull you panties down and sit. Then I'll go get Aunt May to help you."

She did as he commanded and was grateful the oversized T-shirt fell to her thighs.

"Don't fall off of this toilet," he ordered before leaving.

A moment later, Aunt May came in, but since Dixie hadn't had much to expel, she was already wiped and ready to stand.

Aunt May held onto her until Dixie pulled up her panties. Then May called for Dan, who returned to help Dixie into bed.

After Aunt May arranged the pillows, she left to get Dixie something to drink.

Dan sat next to her and brushed her hair from her forehead. "That medicine knocked you out. Are you feeling better?"

She nodded, wanting to speak. It would be easier after she wet her whistle.

Aunt May entered with a quart jar of orange liquid and a straw.

After a few sips, her brain woke up a little. "Just a dull headache. Mainly, I'm lethargic. My muscles are heavy."

"Drink a little more then lay back and rest. The

kids are fine. They're in the pool, and Uncle Ben Hill's the lifeguard, so don't worry."

Dixie wanted to ask why she wasn't in the cottage, but that whole conversation was a distant blur, and she didn't have the energy to put up a fight.

"Thank you for taking care of us," she said and meant it.

If not for Dan, the girls would be on their own caring for her. It had been a while since she'd gotten a migraine. Normally, she could feel it coming in advance and take the medicine in time to stave it off. The previous day had been an exception with the high stress and emotional turmoil. It had hit her like a line drive up the middle, straight between the eyes.

By the next afternoon, Dixie's back could no longer handle lying down. She still struggled to sit on the side of the bed, but she was much better than the day before.

She'd had broth, water, ginger ale, and more orange sports drink too, which had made her trips to the bathroom more frequent. Each time, Dan was by her side, helping her. He only allowed the kids to come see her one at the time. Even Danny, who wasn't her biggest fan, came in to check on her.

"What you need, darlin'?"

This time she couldn't prevent her smile. "A bath. I smell."

He helped her to her feet, but she was able to walk on her on.

"I'm not sure I want you to clean up and get changed."

"Why?"

"Because you look too dang good in my shirt."

She glanced down at the T-shirt and pulled at the hem. "This old thing."

Flirting was a bad idea when a girl looked and smelled as bad as she did. She was lucky he didn't gag and run from the room.

"I'll start the bath water and get Nancy in here to help you."

"Nancy's here?"

"Yeah, she followed us home from the hospital to get you changed and settled. Then today, she brought Sheila over to swim with the kids."

"Those kids are gonna grow fins."

"You should see Maddie. She's so comfortable in the water now."

Dixie's heart smiled at the note of pride in his voice.

Her sister came in to help her into the tub but left her alone to bathe. Dixie soaked her aching back and washed her hair and body. When she emerged from the steamy bathroom in clean clothes, she felt like a new woman.

At the bedroom door, she stopped short, listening as Dan and Nancy laughed together. Her heart clenched with a spasm of envy at hearing her sister and her boss enjoying an easy camaraderie.

Dixie wondered why she'd never thought of it before. Nancy was newly unattached. Her successful attorney sister and her successful businessman boss would make a good match. Nancy had less baggage, and no one would ever accuse her of being a gold-digger.

***

"There she is," Dan said. "You look like you can join the living now, darlin'."

With color back in her cheeks, she was more radiant than ever, causing his old heart to skitter in his chest.

"I feel like I've been asleep for a week," Dixie said.

"I'm glad you're better, Sister. You looked like hell yesterday."

"Felt like it too," Dixie said with a small smile.

"Come sit with us," Dan said.

"Thanks, but I think I might take a short walk to stretch my legs if that's okay."

"Of course, it's okay. We'll join you." Dan stood.

"Oh, I don't want to interrupt." Dixie waved her hand as she headed for the back door. "Y'all keep visiting. I'm good."

"Uh-uh. There's no way I'm letting you wander off and get too tired to get back." Dan moved close and put his arm around her. "Nancy, would you care to take a walk?"

"I really need to round Sheila up and head home. I have a brief due at eight in the morning."

The three of them walked out to the back porch where Nancy gave Dixie a hug while Sheila dried off.

After Nancy and Sheila left, Dan led Dixie down the path to the lake as the kids splashed and screamed hello to Dixie. He was determined to get her away quickly, so the noise wouldn't set her back.

She blew kisses to them and kept his pace.

"Jason has been here all day, and he has a serious crush on your niece," Dan said. "Luckily, Sheila seems like she's used to admiration."

"She is. My little beauty queen Katie has hers and Nancy's beautiful blonde look."

"Katie's a beauty like her mama." Dan squeezed her to his side then let go. "All of your girls are beautiful. Katie's excited about the pageant next weekend, keeps wanting me to ask her interview questions about current events."

"Lord, she'll drive you crazy with that business. If it gets to be too much, please don't let her be a pest."

"Aw, she don't bother me a bit." He hesitated a moment. "Liz tells me she got an offer from Clay Odom to model his designs. You gonna let her do it?"

Dixie flipped her palms up then quickly lowered them. "I don't know. I don't want to push, but I think it would be good for her. She tends to be introverted, like me. What do *you* think?"

"I think it's a good idea. It would get her in front of people without her having to speak. Less pressure than a pageant. It'd also be a new challenge for her."

"I hadn't thought about that. Maybe not intellectually challenging, but intellect isn't everything, right?"

"Right. I mean she does the dancing classes, but this will help with poise and confidence, especially since she opted out of cheerleading after she made the squad."

"That's my fault. I talked her into trying out, and she really didn't want to. The modeling thing will be better, I think. More suited to her personality. Like you said, she won't have to talk in front of people." Dixie stopped and inhaled deeply. "I may need to turn back. I'm a weakling."

"You need to take it easy, darlin'. I need you healthy to help me with all of our children, and I need you at work. That is, if you didn't really quit on me."

She looked down and swallowed hard. "I was angry. I felt betrayed when I saw that report, like you didn't trust me."

He turned to face her. "I trust you more than anyone else in the world. You're honest to a fault. I'm sorry my prying has caused you so much trouble. I'll make it up to you."

"It's not your fault really." She bit her lip.

He thought about whose else's fault it could be. "You blame your husband?"

Her gaze was on the ground in front of her feet, and she gave a small shake of her head but said nothing.

He put his arm around her. "Don't cry, darlin'. I don't want you to make yourself sick. Take a breath. It's nothing we can't handle."

"I don't know what I'd do without you." She leaned into him, placing her palm on his chest.

His heart thumped hard. *You don't have to find out*. He kissed the top of her head. "I feel the same way."

As they neared the house, the children again demanded her attention.

"Mama, look at me." Maddie jumped into the pool.

"Mama D, watch this." A small plastic bag duck taped over Paul's cast kept it dry as he jumped off the diving board.

"Mama!" Katie screamed as she slid down the slide.

"I'm gonna change my name." Dixie grinned as she sat on the edge of the pool and took off her shoes before putting her feet in the water. "Y'all are gonna turn into frogs."

Dan kicked off his shoes and sat beside her.

"Hey, Mama, Mr. Dan, watch me." Katie ran and did a front flip off of the diving board.

"Oh, my goodness, baby." Dixie clapped. "Who taught you that trick?"

"Danny." She dog paddled over to the side near them.

The next thing Dan knew, the children formed a line, waiting for their turn to do a trick off the diving board to impress Mama D.

Dan and Dixie ended up almost as wet as the kids.

The youngsters were happy, and so were the adults as Dixie laughed and applauded, leaning into him to try to avoid getting splashed.

This was the life he wanted. He could never turn his back on it.

Chapter Twenty-eight

Dixie's stomach twisted with nerves as she clutched a bouquet of red roses adorned with baby's breath.

"And the winner is…contestant number eleven, Katherine Marie Johnson."

Everyone on their entire row shot to their feet, whistling and cheering as Katie did her pageant walk across the stage to claim her banner and crown. Her added curtsy, wave, and blown kisses made the rest of the crowd stand and applaud.

Dixie swiped at her eyes and noticed Dan do the same. She wrapped her arms around him and stood on her tiptoes to kiss his cheek. He enveloped her in his arms. At home in his embrace, her heart felt like an overblown balloon.

"I guess our little doll baby isn't going to need these roses since she won a bouquet bigger than she is," he said.

"She'll love them because they're from you. I

think you're her new favorite person."

"Good to know, darlin'. How about you? Who's your favorite person?"

Before she could answer, Nancy put her arms around Dixie and Dan to congratulate them. When she released Dixie, Nancy kept her arm around Dan's neck.

Once again, jealousy and doubt crept into Dixie's mind, and she stepped away to give them space. She made her way to the stage where Liz was snapping Polaroid pictures of Katie in her crown and banner as the official pageant photographer did the same.

"Mama, I won." Katie danced over to the edge of the stage.

"I'm so proud of you, baby." Dixie kissed her cheek.

"Mr. Dan, I won. Look at my crown."

Dixie turned and bumped into Dan. She hadn't realized he'd followed her, and she tried to suppress her smile of pleasure.

"I'm proud as a peacock, doll baby. You're beautiful."

Dixie beamed at the love in his voice, and her heart warmed when he pulled Katie off the stage to hug her then set her back in place.

When Katie ran off to join her fellow winners and runners-up, Dixie asked, "Where did Nancy get off to?"

"She said to tell you she's going backstage to start packing up Katie's things."

"I better go help," Dixie said. "Thank you for coming and supporting her in this."

"I wouldn't have missed it." He squeezed her to his chest.

"Well, it's a good thing you took my advice, Dixie."

They turned to see Tiffany's mom, Cheryl, standing with one hand on her hip and the other holding Tiffany's trophy for second runner-up.

"Advice?" Dan asked.

"Yeah, I told her to take you off the market or else I would." Cheryl leered at him.

"Oh, it's not what you think—" Dixie started.

"Yes. It is." Dan cut her off.

"I see the way you look at each other," Cheryl said. "Anyone with eyes can see it."

"Let 'em look," Dan said.

Dixie wondered if everyone *had* noticed. Looking around the crowded room, she felt the judgmental glances. She and Dan should have been more careful. Her happiness quickly diminished.

Dan swept her away from Cheryl and back to where the boys waited with Maddie. "Oh no, you don't. Don't let her steal your joy, darlin'."

"It's not just her. People are whispering."

He smirked. "Let 'em whisper."

"That's easy for you to say. You're not the one they'll judge."

He stopped and turned to face her. "I guess the only way to salvage what's left of your reputation is for me to make an honest woman of you."

Laughter bubbled up, even though she wanted to be angry. His easy-going demeanor went a long way in balancing out the heavier notes in her personality.

"You're so right. Anything they say is speculation. What they really want to see is a gold-digger. Maybe I'll get one of those cubic zirconia tennis bracelets and start flaunting it around town. When people ask where I got it, I'll be elusive."

"Yeah, right. Ribbing is not your strong suit, but I love that about you. If you want to put on a show for folks, all you have to do is ask. I'll oblige." He wriggled his brows.

"I bet you'd have fun doing it too. You're as slippery as a snake, Dan Baker, but I'm starting to love that about you."

Right then and there, in front of God and everybody, Dan dipped her back and kissed her silly. When people started applauding, he took her a little lower.

"Dad, gross. Stop it," Danny snarled.

"Look, Maddie. They're playing tonsil hockey," Johnny said.

"Daddy, let Mama D breathe," Paul said.

When Dan broke the kiss and righted her, she was breathless and probably red as a cherry. Paul held out his inhaler to her, which made her laugh and bury her face in Dan's chest.

A moment later, she bent down to Paul's level. "Way to think on your feet. I don't need it right now, but thanks for the offer." She hugged him close and pecked his cheek.

He slipped his arms around her neck and squeezed tight. "I love you, Mama D."

"I love you too, cutie." She stood with him in her arms.

It was clear he missed having a mama to hold

him. Dixie wanted so much to fill the void for him.
***

Dan thought his heart and his zipper would explode. Between the kiss and Dixie loving on his baby boy, Dan really was ready to make her his.

"I've got to go get Katie." Dixie put Paul down.

"I'll take this crew to the Suburban," Dan said. "Lizabelle, come on, honey." He herded them out to the new car that could accommodate them all.

Maddie spoke in a loud whisper. "They were kissing, Lizabelle. Do you think Mama liked it?"

Dan pressed his lips together a second, but eventually quit fighting the smile which was dying to break out. "I hope she liked it, sugar. If she says different, you tell Big Dan, and I'll see if I can do it better next time. I'm kinda out of practice."

"So's Mama," Maddie said. "Y'all can practice together."

"Y'all, Mama's gonna be so embarrassed." Liz shook her head.

"How come?" Maddie asked.

"Because grown up kissing is private, and she wouldn't want us talking about it."

"But they did it in pub...pub... What's that word?"

"Public," Dan said. "I shouldn't have kissed your mama in public. It might make her mad."

"But she was happy," Maddie said.

"Yeah," Paul said. "Mama D was laughing. I think she liked it. Way to go, Daddy."

"Oh hell." Dan ran a hand through his hair. "Your mama *is* gonna kill me."

"She might be a little embarrassed," Liz said. "But she won't kill you."

"What would you kids think if—"

"Dad, don't." Danny held up his hand. "It's not up to us, so no need to plant seeds."

Liz rolled her eyes at Danny. "You're such a know-it-all."

"You're one to talk, smarty-pants," Danny shot back.

"One day, when I sign your paycheck, I'm gonna remind you of this moment," she said.

"Ain't no damn way I'd ever work for a woman, much less you," Danny said.

"Son," Dan said. "I *will* beat your ass right here in public. What have I told you about how you speak to women? Would you talk to your mama that way?"

"No, sir."

"I get that you're upset. I get that you miss your mama, but you cannot, you *will* not, take out your frustrations on every female that enters your life. You have to get control of yourself and your temper, and you *have* to learn to respect women. You will treat every last one of them as if she were your mother in another skin. You hear me?"

"Yes, sir."

"Danny." Maddie grabbed his hand. "A real man never hurts a woman, even with words. God made a woman out of a man's rib. It's here, in your side." She poked him, and he pulled back concealing a grin. "It's kind of under your arm, so you can protect them, and close to your heart, so you can love them."

"How did you get so smart?" Danny towered over little Maddie.

"Lizabelle read it to me in one of her books."

Danny made a face before he looked at Liz. "I'm sorry, Lizzz...abelle."

Turning his head, Dan wiped his eyes. It was funny how the youngest kid in the bunch seemed to be the wisest.

"Mr. Dan," Katie sang his name as she raced across the parking lot toward him. She had changed into a casual outfit but still wore her crown and sash.

Dixie followed with an armload of clothes and flowers, and Nancy was right behind her, carrying a tote bag full of makeup and other beauty supplies.

Dan had just scooped Katie into his arms when the squealing of tires drew his attention. A late model Cadillac barreled down the circular drive.

Dixie and Nancy were right in its path.

Dan set Katie down and ran full speed. He held his arms straight out and picked up both women around their waists, using his momentum to slam them onto the asphalt, out of the path of the car.

The car swerved and slowed after missing its target. Then it burned rubber off of school property.

From his position on the ground, Dan hovered over Dixie, his blood rushing forcefully through his head. "Darlin', are you okay? Say something."

She drew in a sharp breath. "That was some tackle, Big Dan. I hope the scouts were watching."

He placed light kisses all over her face. "I thought I was gonna lose you."

"Somebody needs to revoke that guy's driver's

license," Dixie said.

Nancy knelt beside them. "I don't think that was a careless driver, Sister. He was gunning for one of us."

Dan sent Cheryl inside to call the police. While they waited, he held Dixie close and rubbed her neck and back, guilt eating at him.

"I'm sorry I hit you so hard, darlin'."

"You didn't hit me as hard as the car would've." She put her palm on his cheek. "Relax, sweetheart, I'm fine."

He saw it then—the look in her eyes, the love. He was a goner, and in response, he kissed her fiercely.

When he realized he was being too rough, he lightened his touch before he pulled away.

She sighed. "It's a good thing we're in public."

"Uh-huh. Why's that, darlin?"

"Because I have a hard time controlling my hormones when you kiss me like that."

"I'm sorry if I was…indelicate."

"You weren't indelicate. You were…" A grin formed on her pretty face. "Dan-ly." She wriggled her eyebrows.

Heat flashed through him. "I like the sound of that."

Chapter Twenty-nine

After dealing with the police, Dixie stretched her neck and massaged some of the tension out of her shoulders. She couldn't wait to get home—well, her temporary home—to take a relaxing shower.

Since the sheriff hadn't caught the arsonist yet, she and the girls were still staying in the cottage at Southland. She had to admit Southland provided a safe haven, even before Dan had had a giant security gate installed. He'd let the kids, hers and his, pick out the lettering design for the name over the gate. They'd unanimously chose the Western font. The eighteen-inch tall iron letters spread across the twenty foot span of the entrance to Southland, alerting all visitors they'd arrived.

"Nancy," Dan said. "Since Sheila's staying with friends tonight, why don't you come stay with us? Just in case the crazy driver was angry with you over a case or something."

"Thanks, but I can't impose. You already have

a half-dozen munchkins and my sister to look after."

Dixie's heart dropped to the pavement.

"Don't say it like they're a burden to me."

Dan's brow furrowed. "They're not. I love each and every one of those girls like they're my own."

The corners of Nancy's mouth slowly turned up into a smile, triumph written all over her face.

"It's high time you admitted it, Big Dan." Nancy winked at Dixie. "I'll come out and stay with my sister tonight."

Relief and disappointment battled for top emotion in Dixie's mind. Dan had stoked her fire with his luscious lip-smacking, and she'd hoped for privacy later. But in case Nancy was in danger, Dixie wanted her safe at home with them.

"Come on, Sister." Dixie tugged Nancy's arm toward their parked cars.

"Mama, can we watch TV at the main house?" Liz asked, getting out of the car at Southland.

The cottage didn't have a television.

"Daddy, I'm hungry," Johnny said.

"I think midnight breakfast is in order," Dan said. "Aunt May's probably in bed, so we'll have to put her kitchen back in order when we're finished."

The kids cheered, and Dan put a VHS movie on for them while Dixie and Nancy started preparing the food. Dan joined them and took over bacon duty, so Dixie could crack and whip the eggs. Nancy started the grits, but Dixie laughed as her sister read the directions on the package.

"Here, Sister." Dixie took the boiler, filled it

with water, and added salt. "When it boils, put two cups of grits in there and stir."

"No fair. You learned all of the domestic skills from taking care of Daddy," Nancy said.

Dixie nodded. "I tried to take some of the load off of Mama's shoulders."

"I hated that for you." Nancy grimaced. "Kids shouldn't have to be responsible for their parents."

"I didn't mind. I learned to cook, which I might not have if Daddy had been well."

"You're right," she said. "He would've kept all of us on horseback until we were bowlegged."

Dixie chuckled. Their dad had been severely bowlegged and had said it was from being on horses all his life.

"Things do work out sometimes, don't they?" Dixie asked. "You found the law in the mess. I found my niche, too."

Dan hugged Dixie from behind and ran his hands up and down her arms.

Nancy smirked as she put the lid on the pot of grits. "You definitely found your niche, Sister."

Dixie had found her home in Dan's arms. The concerns from weeks before about mixing business and pleasure were slowly fading away since each day she fell a little deeper in love with the man she'd tried to use for a one-time adventure.

"I think I like you cooking in my kitchen," Dan said.

"Don't get used to it," Dixie teased. "I'm a career woman, and I work for a tyrant."

"Hmm. I'll have to have a little talk with that boss of yours." He moved away to check the bacon.

"D, when's the conference?" Nancy asked, taking a seat at the table. "Are you still going?"

Dixie regarded Dan. "We're waiting to see if things settle down here. I'm still booked to go, but I don't want to leave the girls if there's danger."

"I'll come out and stay with the kids if that's okay with you, Dan," Nancy offered.

Another pang of jealous irritation hit Dixie. She couldn't figure out if Nancy had a crush on Dan or not. And the idea of them spending a long weekend together while she was halfway across the country all alone did not sit well. If Nancy weren't between men, it wouldn't bother Dixie so much, but Nancy changed men like she changed nail polish. And her sister had a standing weekly appointment at the nail salon in Bull Creek.

"That's a great idea," Dan said. "I'm sure it would make D feel a lot better about leaving the girls."

A disparaging snort escaped Dixie, and she pounded her fist on her chest, covering it with a cough. "Excuse me."

"Do you want to shop in my closet for something to wear on your trip? I mean, you have to take in a few shows and fawn over the Elvis impersonators."

"Are we talking young Elvis or old Elvis?" she asked.

"You'll see all kinds, every race, size, and sex."

Dixie cackled. "Female Elvises?"

"Stay away from Elvis," Dan said. "You'll be working, and I won't have you fondling the King on my dime." He pressed his lips together and turned away, but not before she caught his grin.

"Well, I wouldn't fondle him...not on the first date."

"Uh-huh." Dan smirked. "Like you didn't fondle me on our first date."

Dixie's face burned, and Nancy nearly fell out of her chair, giggling like a schoolgirl.

Dixie thrust her chin in the air. "That wasn't a date." She pointed to the stove. "Your bacon's burning."

"My bacon was burning that night, too."

"Cut it out." Dixie swatted at him with the spoon she'd used to scramble the eggs.

Egg landed on Dan's cheek. His eyes bulged at the same time his jaw dropped open. His expression was priceless, and Dixie doubled over, howling with laughter.

"Have a little egg on your face there, Dan?" Nancy asked when she'd recovered from chortling.

Dan narrowed his eyes and slowly wiped his face with his knuckles. He looked at his fingers then put them in his mouth. "Mmm. Tasty."

"You're gonna get me back, aren't you?" Dixie stepped away slowly.

She dropped the spoon and turned to run for the safety of the living room and the protection of the kids. Before she could get there, he caught up to her and lifted her into his arms. He set her down on the second step of the stairwell, where they were eye to eye.

In the intimacy of the moment, everything tightened inside. With his hands firmly holding her face, she melted deep into his kiss. She snaked her arms around his neck, and he pressed himself into her, laying over her on the stairs. A little moan of pleasure escaped her throat as she lost herself.

Coughing drew her awareness away from Dan, and she opened her eyes.

Dan hadn't heard it or was ignoring it, so she placed her hands on his shoulders and gently pushed. Just beyond him, a dozen eyeballs watched with varying degrees of emotions.

"Did you fall up the stairs, Daddy?" Johnny asked.

"And take Mama D down with you?" Danny asked with an added note of skepticism.

***

Dan couldn't believe his ears. He wanted to shout to the rooftops because Danny had called Dixie Mama D, but making a big deal out of it would be a huge mistake.

Dan's heart was ready to burst at the seams, so he got to his feet and pulled Dixie up with him. "Breakfast is ready, kids."

As he took his seat at the head of the table, he smiled at the easy banter of the children. They were already like family, so he didn't think any of them would have a problem with him marrying Dixie. The exception might've been Danny, but Dixie seemed to be winning him over slowly.

Dan wondered if Dixie would say the same about him. Seated to his right, he reached under the table and squeezed her hand.

Her eyes widened and she hopped up. "Oh, my goodness. I almost forgot the biscuits."

After going into the kitchen, she returned with a large bowl of biscuits in one hand and butter and Mayhaw jelly in the other. If there was one thing Dan loved, it was a good biscuit swimming in Aunt May's Mayhaw jelly.

One bite sealed the deal.

"You've got to marry me now that I've tasted your hot biscuits," he said.

Dixie narrowed her eyes at him.

Nancy slapped his free arm. "If you're trying to propose, you've got to do better than that."

"Sorry." He chewed a mouthful of the warm, chewy, delectable treat. "My stomach spoke for me."

"I'm with Dad on this one." Danny wiped jelly from his chin. "But don't tell Aunt May."

"Yeah," Johnny said. "Y'all should get married."

"Yeah," Katie, Maddie, and Paul said in unison.

"Lizabelle," Dan said, "you haven't weighed in yet."

"That's because it's not my decision. If you're asking me, you're asking the wrong person." Liz cut her eyes back to her plate.

"Wise child." Dixie raised an eyebrow at Dan.

"What? Don't tell me we wouldn't be great together. Just look at our family." He gestured his hand down the length of the table. "I love your girls, and I want to adopt them…if you'll let me."

"Yeah, Daddy, and Mama D can adopt us too," Johnny said.

Dixie closed her eyes and dropped her head

into her palms as she sucked in a deep breath.

"I know I'm going about this all wrong, but I'd like you to be my wife." The confidence in his tone overrode the desperation in his chest.

"Oh, yeah?" she asked, her lips forming a tight line as she glared at him. "Well, I'd like to love and be loved by the next man I marry. All I've ever heard from you is how much you love my girls. That's wonderful, but their father loved them too, and he didn't love me. I refuse to live like that again. I'm sorry to disappoint you all."

She threw her napkin down and faced the kids. "But the answer is no."

Chapter Thirty

It took all of Dixie's strength to calmly get out of her chair and walk out the back door. She was a selfish woman, denying her girls every chance for happiness. A hot tear ran down her cheek, and she swiped it with the back of her hand as she headed down the path to the lake.

It had to be wrong to want love when she was raising three girls by herself. The more she thought about it, the more she realized she hadn't been entirely alone lately. Dan had been there for every disaster and every victory, holding her hand all the while.

Maybe he did love her. But maybe, it was just pity. His generous spirit might be confusing the two. She didn't want to be another one of his charity cases.

On the other hand, she couldn't deny their attraction to each other…and the affection in his eyes. She was the biggest fool. Turning abruptly, to run back to the house, she ran into a brick wall of muscle.

"Ow," she said as his strong hands gripped her back.

"What's wrong, darlin'?" He lightened his grasp.

"My back's tender. Probably from the close call with the concrete earlier…or the stairs."

"I'm so sorry, Dixie. You have to know I didn't mean to hurt you, physically or otherwise."

"I know. You're a good man, and you'd never intentionally hurt me or my girls, even if you don't mind manipulating us all a little bit—"

"I didn't mean—"

"Shh." She placed a finger on his lips. "Let me talk for once."

The corners of his mouth turned up.

"I have to hear it, Dan. Straight from here."

"Dad," Danny ran up to them with a shotgun in one hand and a revolver in the other, "Deputy Cook called and said there's a Cadillac parked on the road."

Dan took the revolver. "Let's get Dixie back to the house. You stay inside and protect our family, Danny. Hide, turn off the lights, and send Ben Hill down. Make sure he's armed."

"Yes, sir."

Dan took one of Dixie's arms, and Danny took the other as they jogged back to the house, all the while looking around in the darkness for danger. Once on the porch, Dan pushed her toward the back door, and Danny pulled her inside the house.

"I already sent the kids upstairs to the

playroom." Danny didn't release his grip on her until they'd joined the others.

Aunt May sat on the couch, hugging and rocking Paul and Maddie. Liz was leaning against the wall with Johnny and Katie in each arm, Nancy beside them. Danny closed the door, turned out the light, and moved to the window to peep out from behind the curtain.

Dixie's pulse thumped loudly at the base of her skull as she leaned against the door and slid down to the floor. "Girls, pray for Mr. Dan and Uncle Ben Hill."

"Okay." Quiet voices cut the thick air in the room as boys and girls joined to ask for safety for their loved ones.

***

Dan peered around the corner of the house, straining his ears toward the front of the property. A noise behind him forced him to swing around, pistol in hand.

Uncle Ben Hill crept along the stone exterior with two flashlights in one hand and a sawed-off shotgun in the other. "Dat sum gun dun picked on da wrong folks."

Dan fisted his shirt in his hand over his chest and let out a loud breath. "You got that right, Uncle."

After taking a flashlight, Dan held it with his finger poised over the switch. It would give away his location, so he wouldn't turn it on unless he needed to.

While Ben Hill shuffled off to the other side of the driveway, Dan moved to the edge of the trees at the front of the house. He knew Southland like the back of his hand, but a stranger would get lost in his woods. In all likelihood, the trespasser would stick to one of the footpaths.

With only pale moonlight for visibility, Dan carefully picked his way through the trees, watching the shadowy ground a few feet in front of him for anything which might make noise if he stepped on it. At the same time, he listened, occasionally scanning the area for signs of the intruder.

On the horse trail about five feet to his left, a limb snapped. Dan narrowed his eyes.

A squishy noise was followed by a foul word. A brief flash of light lit up the night then went out again.

The man scrubbed the bottom of his shoe on a nearby tree, the sound loud in the otherwise eerie quiet. Road apples made for a good distraction.

Dan aimed his gun and flashlight toward the intruder. "Freeze." For a brief second, he was proud of himself for sounding so confident and official.

A shot rang out, and Dan squeezed the trigger as fire burned through him. He tried to take a step, but pain sent him to his knees. He repositioned the beam of light to see a man crumpled on the ground a few feet away.

Dan let out his loudest whistle, and moments later, footsteps approached at a run.

"Big Dan!" Deputy Cook called.

The sound of a leather gun belt rubbing against a holster grew louder.

"I think I got him, Bob." Something warm and viscous trickled down Dan's left leg.

Ben Hill's steel-toe boots thudded, shaking the ground until he knelt next to Dan.

***

Dixie bolted upright at the sound of gunfire. When she reached for the door, Danny's hand covered hers on the knob.

"I can't protect everyone if you run out of here and split us up." Danny's words were followed by an audible swallow.

"Oh, honey. You're much too young to be responsible for so many."

"No, I'm not." His tone wasn't defiant, just confident.

"Miss Dixie!"

The alarm in Ben Hill's voice made Danny release her hand, and as soon as she cleared the door, she bolted down the stairs, taking two at a time. She ignored the soreness in her back muscles.

Ben Hill and Deputy Cook were laying Dan on the dining table.

"He dun got hisself shot."

Cries and screams chorused from the kids behind her.

"Kids, he's gonna be fine." Dixie slid plates from the uncleared table to one end to make more room. "Nancy, take them into the living room and say a prayer. Deputy, call an ambulance."

"Already did, ma'am."

"Aunt May, grab the first aid kit." The blood was radiating from his left hip. "I need scissors or a knife."

She held out her hand, and an instant later, Ben

Hill placed a heavy hunting knife in her palm. She cut the fabric away and began cleaning the area with the gauze Aunt May handed her.

"Help me lift him," she said. "I need to see if the bullet went through."

There was no exit wound, which could be good or bad depending on where the bullet had lodged.

Dan moaned and jerked his knee as they lowered him back down.

Dixie put light pressure on the entry wound and moved closer to his head. She brushed his hair from his forehead. "Be still, sweetheart. I'm gonna take care of you."

She kissed his lips before she returned to his wound, amazing herself because she'd switched from woman mode to nurse mode in the blink of an eye.

"Mama D, can I help?" Danny asked.

"Hold pressure right here for me, honey." She looked through the first aid kit for an antimicrobial agent.

The best she could do at the moment was slow the blood loss and clean the area. If she knew the trajectory of the bullet, she might be able to go after it, but she couldn't risk damaging his organs and him bleeding out on her.

"Stay with me, Dan," she whispered close to his ear, not wanting to upset Danny.

In the distance, a siren ripped through the air, and she let out a long, forced breath. "He's gonna be okay, Danny. Do you want to ride with him to the hospital? I'll follow in my car."

"Yes'm."

In a whirlwind of activity, the medics came in, put Dan on a gurney, and whisked him out again. She appreciated their expediency.

Before she left, she detoured to the living room to speak to the children.

"Mama D." Paul sobbed and hiccupped. "You'll take care of Daddy, won't you? Even if you don't want to marry him?"

"Of course I will, cutie." She hugged him close. "I love your daddy, and I love you too. If he asks me again, I won't say no. I promise."

The grin on his face was worth the wait to get to the hospital.

"I've got to run. Aunt May, I'm sorry about the mess in the kitchen."

"I'll clean it up, Mama." Liz stood.

"Don't cha worry your pretty head, Miss Dixie. You go on and see about Dan."

"Did they get the bad guy?" Johnny asked.

"Your daddy shot him," Deputy Cook said from the doorway.

"I'm glad," Katie said. "That bad man needed shootin'."

Dixie didn't have the time or energy to correct her daughter, and the truth was she felt the same way, but courtesy dictated she never say such a thing aloud.

"I love you. All of you." She hugged and kissed the kids, her sister, and Aunt May before she grabbed her purse and rushed out the door.

Chapter Thirty-one

The smell of antiseptic burned Dan's nose, and he snapped his eyes open. The bright light above the bed seared his retinas, so he clamped them shut again.

"Dad?" Danny shook Dan's shoulder. "Dad, are you awake?"

The second time Dan was more cautious, squinting until he could see his eldest son's face and the concern etched in the tightness around his mouth.

He cleared his throat. "Did I get him?"

"Yes, sir. He's deader than a doornail."

"I didn't mean to kill 'em." His rusty voice made him sound a million years old.

"It was dark, and it was self-defense." Danny glanced at a sheet of paper in his hand. "They found accelerant," he pronounced the word carefully, "in the trunk of the car, so they're pretty sure it's the same guy who burned Mama D's house down."

"Well, I reckon I'm glad the bastard's dead then."

"Dan." Dixie approached from the other side and took his hand. "While I appreciate your protectiveness, you have to be careful what you say."

"Why?" He turned his head for a look at her. "Why not say what you think? You may not lie outright, Dixie, but you sure bite your tongue enough to conceal the truth. That's just as bad as lying in my book."

"Okay." She let go of him. "The doctor asked me to get him when you wake up."

Before he could speak up and stop her, she darted out of the room. He hadn't meant to lash out at her, especially since she was probably responsible for him being alive.

"Call Nancy, son. I need her to take care of some legal stuff for me posthaste."

"It's Sunday, and she's still at Southland helping with the kids."

"Call her quick. Before Dixie gets back."

A few minutes later, Dan hung up the receiver on the heavy rotary phone as the door opened and Dixie entered, followed by a man in a white coat.

"Dan, this is Dr. Carson. He performed the surgery to remove the bullet."

"Mr. Baker, I'm glad to see you awake and alert." He shown a bright light into Dan's eyes and checked his vitals. "The good news is the bullet missed your major organs and lodged in your pelvis. A few weeks of therapy and you'll be back on your feet."

"But Doc, I need to be on my feet sooner than that. I have a half-dozen kids to look after."

Once again, Dan realized he'd stuck his foot in it when Dixie shook her head and walked out of the room.

"You should be thankful you still have all of your parts, Mr. Baker. I thought telling you you'd need a few weeks of therapy would be a better alternative to your never having kids, but since you have six already, I'm guessing you're ready to slow down."

Dan had never considered having more children. In his mind, a half-dozen crumbsnatchers and a Baker's dozen grandkids down the road sounded like a good plan.

The problem was the mother of their kids didn't seem very interested in committing herself to him, but he only had himself to blame for that.

***

Dixie was asleep on her feet, so she detoured to the coffee pot at the nurse's station.

"Are you avoiding me or what?"

Startled by the voice, she burnt her hand as she overshot the cup. She grabbed for paper towels, but Dr. Flint took them and unrolled a few. He took her cup and set it on the counter as he dried and examined her hand.

"I didn't mean to scare you."

"Oh, it's nothing. I'm sorry I've been out of touch. Things have been crazy with me."

He filled her coffee cup and made one for himself. "Tell me."

As they sat at the small table in the lounge and

sipped their hot beverages, she filled him in on the events of the previous night.

"So, you haven't been staying at the rental? I thought not because I've been by a few times and no one was home."

"I'm sorry, Ron. You must think I'm such a mess."

"Not at all. I see a strong, beautiful woman playing with the cards she was dealt. In fact, I think you stepped up to the table after the cards were dealt and got someone else's shitty hand."

Dixie's coffee nearly came out of her nose as she laughed, and her eyes stung because his words so clearly expressed the way she'd felt since Steve died.

She forced back the tears and contrived a smile. "Thank you for the vote of confidence. It's nice to hear every now and again that I'm not a complete failure at my life."

The more time she spent in Dr. Flint's presence the more comfortable she felt in her own skin. He made her feel like she could do anything instead of constantly reminding her that she was better with a man at her side to support her.

"God made woman to be a helpmate, a partner for man. He never intended for either to go it alone." Her daddy's voice rang crystal clear, breaking into her thoughts as if he were standing right next to her.

Chill bumps pimpled her arms, but when she glanced around, her father wasn't there.

A lump rose in her throat. Alone. She'd been married for a decade, most of which she'd spent battling loneliness. What good was a man if he didn't help you back?

The warmth of Ron's hand covering hers snapped her back to the conversation.

"You're not a failure, Dixie. You're strong. And you can and will do whatever needs to be done. I'm here if you need me."

The stark contrast of his offer of help compared to Dan's helping without asking hit her like a Cadillac out of control. But Dan knew she wouldn't ask.

Sometimes, she hated how well he knew her.

One thing he didn't know how to do was propose…or tell her he loved her. Her beat-up old heart longed to hear it, even if it wasn't true.

Chapter Thirty-two

Getting up the narrow stairs of the jet was difficult with crutches, but Dan was determined. As soon as he'd settled into his seat for the flight to Las Vegas, the pilot exchanged the walking aids for a glass of scotch.

Dan owed his buddy, Frank, for the free ride to Nevada. If things went according to plan, Dan would buy his own jet to take the missus wherever she wanted to go, anytime.

As the liquid burned a path down his throat, he thought back to his last therapy appointment a few days earlier when he'd pitched a natural born fit, cussing and slinging the crutches across the room.

"You don't understand. I have to be able to walk down the aisle when I get married this weekend."

"Mr. Baker, can't you just postpone the ceremony for a few weeks? I'm sure your fiancée would understand." The young man who'd been helping with his physical therapy cast his gaze to the floor.

Dan didn't have a fiancée yet, and if he wasn't man enough to stand on his own two feet, he'd never convince Dixie to marry him. Who would want to marry a cripple?

Pleading, Dan pinned the young man with a sorrowful stare. "Isn't there anything I can do?"

He twisted his mouth. "You'll need your crutches...and ask her to be gentle. I mean, how can you have a wedding night if—"

"I get it. How can I please my bride if I can't perform?" Dan hadn't thought through that little problem.

How could he expect her to postpone their wedding night? How could he ask her to be his if he couldn't satisfy her? How could he even convince her to say yes?

After patting his front pocket for the umpteenth time, he relaxed in his seat. The little velvet box was still there, waiting to be opened to reveal its contents to its mistress.

He may not be at one hundred percent, but by God, he was still more man than he'd ever come across, and he aimed to prove it to Dixie.

Once he arrived at The Dunes, he'd head straight to the front desk to sort a few things out.

***

At the Atlanta airport, Dixie hesitated with her hand on the inside door handle of her sister's Mercedes.

Dixie had changed her mind about the trip to Las Vegas a dozen times, especially since she'd dreamed about snakes in the desert three nights in a row. The only thing the premonition really told her was that the danger would be in Nevada, not near her family in Georgia.

The unanswered questions in Dixie's mind revolved around whether the bookie had hired the arsonist and the hit and run driver. Did he want Dixie scared…or dead?

Her thoughts returned to the present when Nancy handed Dixie a file folder of business papers and practically pushed her out of the car. "Read these on your flight."

"You expect me to be able to concentrate on anything other than my first plane ride and being suspended thousands of feet up in the air?" She swallowed back her panic.

"People fly every day. You'll be fine. Have a great trip, Sister. I love you."

Dixie wrinkled her nose and gathered her luggage. "Love you too. Thanks for helping out with the girls while I'm gone."

The first class seat was spacious, and once settled, she stared out of the small window to avoid the gazes of the coach class patrons passing by. In truth, she was coach class and was sure all the passengers knew it. Dan, on the other hand, was first class all the way.

Dixie needed to accept she might never live up to the standards of the well-to-do. She was just a simple country girl with good nursing skills and an extrasensory awareness of certain things.

"Is this seat taken?"

Dixie looked up to find Ron Flint hovering in

the aisle.

"I'm not sure." She allowed a small smile to form. "Let me see your ticket."

Sure enough, as fate would have it, Dr. Flirt was seated next to her for the direct flight to Las Vegas.

She shoved the file folder into her oversized purse. It would have to wait.

Having Ron as a seat partner turned out to be a good thing because he kept Dixie calm during takeoff by making her laugh. The flight attendant brought Champagne, and by the time they touched down in Sin City, Dixie was more than a little tipsy from the bubbly.

They shared a taxi to The Dunes, and when Dixie stepped out, her gaze followed the high-rise hotel to the top.

Once they checked in, Ron asked the bellman to take their luggage up to their rooms.

"Come on." He pulled Dixie's arm. "The sun'll go down soon, and the lights on the Strip are phenomenal."

Reluctantly, Dixie followed her tour guide who was like a kid in a candy store. Since his enthusiasm was contagious, it didn't take her long to loosen up and enjoy the evening.

***

Dixie stretched then snuggled back under the covers next to Dan. His warm body spooned her from behind. When she remembered he shouldn't be lying on his side, her eyes popped open. He was still healing from the gunshot wound.

Sitting up in bed, she pulled the sheet tight over

her bare chest. "What the…"

"Mornin', beautiful."

Dixie shrieked and jumped out of bed, taking the covers with her and in the process, exposing Ron Flint in all his naked majesty. He put both hands behind his head as he arched his back and made a show of stretching.

After checking the clock on the nightstand, he said, "Come back to bed. It's still early."

"Did we?" Dixie pressed her palm against her chest where her heart pounded unsteadily. "Ron, what happened last night?"

He propped up on his elbows. "What do you think happened? Do you really not remember?"

"No, I don't."

"Careful. My fragile ego might not be able to take being so easily forgotten. Come back to bed, and I'll remind you just how much you liked it."

Dixie glanced around the room and spotted her clothes neatly folded, resting on the armchair. "I've got to go."

"Don't forget," Ron said. "Dinner tonight and we have tickets to see Tom Jones. Give me those covers."

"Um, I'll be right back." She dressed in the bathroom and swallowed the bile burning the back of her throat.

How could she have no memory of sex with Ron?

After the plane ride, she hadn't had very much to drink. Nothing like the margarita incident with Dan she'd not soon be forgetting. In fact, she didn't have the typical hangover—not like the hellacious one she'd had after her trip to Margaritaville.

Something was off.

Before she left the bathroom, she checked the trash can for signs of used condoms. It was empty.

Dizziness swamped her, and she gripped the edges of the sink to catch her balance.

Finding the courage to face him again, she flung open the door and found Ron asleep. She had questions, but she wanted to get away to the safety of her own space, so she could think.

She returned the covers to the bed while fighting the urge to kill the man with her bare hands. Then she made her escape.

In her room, she set her purse on the chair and opened her suitcase for clean clothes. She hadn't even been in her room before that moment and guilt slammed into her like Ali's fist into Frazier's face.

She glanced around the room and noted a beautiful vase of bluebells on the nightstand, one of her favorites. Her father grew them and often presented the blooms as tokens of affection to her mother. These must have been complimentary from the hotel. It was a pretty nice place.

When she showered, she checked herself. It didn't feel like she'd had sex, at least not like it had after a night with Dan.

Another left hook packed with guilt made her cover her eyes in shame.

Dan could never know about her night with Ron. It was a good thing he was home in Georgia. She needed a few days to get over what she'd done. Maybe longer.

A thought made her check her tummy and her

backside before she cleaned them thoroughly with soap. Sometimes, men made their deposits outside the female body, but she found no evidence Ron had done that.

No condoms, no sticky stuff, no soreness. It didn't add up.

Pounding on the exterior door nearly scared the pee out of her. She turned off the shower, put on the Dunes' fluffy terrycloth robe, and padded to the door.

"Who is it?"

"Thank God." Dan's voice held more than a hint of relief. "It's me. Are you okay?"

She took a shaky breath before she opened the door to find him standing in front of her, supported by crutches.

"Oh my God," she said. "Are you crazy? What are you doing here? You could get hurt and suffer a setback." She helped him into the room and over to the chair.

"I'm here to surprise you, darlin', but the joke was on me. You must have passed out hard when you got here. I've been calling and knocking since yesterday evenin'."

"Um, yeah, I guess." Her face burned as she stuttered. She couldn't meet his gaze. "Will you be okay for a minute? I wasn't finished showering."

Just as she closed the bathroom door, her mouth soured as she heard his words.

"I hope the flowers made you feel at home."

***

Dan got up to turn on the television and smiled. The florist had done a nice job with the arrangement. Bluebells reminded him of Dixie. Not only because of her eyes but also because the flower was a symbol of everlasting love, the thing he wanted most to share with her.

The hair dryer drowned out the newscaster's voice, and a moment later, the phone rang.

Dan hopped over to the bed on one foot and answered.

"Dixie, you sound like shit," a man said.

"Who the hell's this?" Dan asked.

"Oh, I'm sorry, I must have misdialed. Excuse—"

"You didn't misdial. This is Dan Baker."

"Answering Dixie's room phone? Hmm." A few seconds of silence ticked by. "This is Ron Flint. She didn't tell me she had an early meeting with her boss when she snuck out of my room this morning. I was going to take her to breakfast, but it seems you're a step ahead of me. Tell her not to forget our dinner plans."

Dan gripped the receiver tightly, imagining his hand was around Ron Flint's neck.

The bathroom door opened and Dixie emerged, eyes on the floor as she crossed to her suitcase. She jumped as he slammed the receiver down.

"Do you need something?" she asked. "I can call for you—"

"Hand me my crutches, won't ya?"

She gave them to him and tried to help him up.

"I don't need your help." The words were sharp to his own ears.

"Okay." She backed away to give him space, still not looking at him.

He clomped to the door, and she reached for the handle.

"Ron called." He looked back and watched her cheeks turn pink. "It's true then."

"What's true?" She lifted her chin defiantly.

"You spent the night with him."

Her lower lip quivered and tears welled in her eyes as she sucked in a breath.

"I can't stand the sight of you right now. Do you have one-night stands with every man you meet?" He didn't wait for an answer but stomped down the hall as best as he could with the knife protruding from his back.

He couldn't understand how she'd fooled him. It must have been part of her game all along—to land a rich husband, one way or another. Gold-digger.

In his room, he sat on the bed and rubbed his chest, trying to quell the aching of his heart.

He dialed home. "Uncle Ben Hill, I need you and Aunt May to pack up Dixie's and the girls' things and return them to their rental house. If I'm not mistaken, Nancy has a key."

"What's dis 'bout, Big Dan?"

"I made a mistake."

"Dem little girls gonna be heartbroken."

"Welcome them to my world." He hung up, not wanting to explain himself any further.

His heart hurt not only for the loss of Dixie and what they could have shared, but he truly loved the girls too. He had a lot to answer for to them and his boys.

He dialed Nancy. "Did you give Dixie the

papers?"

"Yes, I told her to read them on the plane."

"That might explain some things," he said. "I should've given it to her *after* I proposed. Would you be insulted to get a prenuptial agreement from a man before he even popped the question?"

"When you put it like that...but, haven't you proposed a bunch of times? What's going on?"

"I never did it right, and now she's moved on." Dan growled at his own dumbassedness as he ran a hand though his hair.

"Impossible."

"She as much as admitted to spending the night with Ron Flint...after he told me about it."

"Wait, what? She wouldn't—"

"Like she wouldn't sleep with me the first night she met me. She didn't even know who I was. I think your sister has fooled you, too."

"If I remember right, you never even asked her name until after you screwed her in the backseat of your truck, you hypocritical asshole. I'm going to get my sister's shit from Southland. Oh, and by the way, I wrote a little loophole into her employment contract. I hope you read it carefully. It basically says if you try to screw her over, you'll bend over and take it up the tailpipe, buddy."

Dan pulled the phone away from his ear as the deafening crack of the receiver on her end caused temporary auditory damage. He'd messed up so much he wasn't sure his world would ever be right again.

He took a Vicodin to stave off the throbbing in his hip and headed for the nearest bar.

Chapter Thirty-three

After Dixie cried every tear her body could produce, she called the airline. The price to change the ticket was more than she wanted to pay, but when she tried, she was told there were no seats available.

She wondered if Dan was in his room pulling little puppet strings to make her life a living hell.

She never wanted to see him again...or Ron Flint for that matter. Men were only good for one thing, and neither of those men had done it for her. At least not in a long time in Dan's case.

The sting of betrayal on his face had cut her to the quick. But the anguish in her heart was quickly turning into anger. She should march down to his room right now and give him a piece of her mind. She should remind him he'd never told her he loved her, that he'd only ever suggested marriage as a joke.

If she were honest with herself, she'd never

told him how she felt either, except when he was unconscious. It was for the best. He'd never know how her own irresponsible behavior with Ron had crushed her dream of a life with Dan. The dream she had just begun to allow to take form in her heart.

She glanced at the clock then out the window. It was a cloudless day if she didn't count the gray cloud over her head. She wanted a drink, but she didn't know if she'd get served at nine in the morning. Besides, she'd obviously had too much the night before.

After considering all her options, she decided to do what she'd come for in the first place—attend the darn conference.

While in a lecture about pain management for late stage cancer patients, she sat next to a female doctor. Impressed by the beautiful woman who'd grown up in India and overcome sexism, racism, and prejudice to achieve her dreams, Dixie made a fast friend.

During one of the breaks, she gathered her courage. "Listen. I know this is going to sound strange, but since you're a gynecologist…could you tell based on a physical examination the morning after if a woman had had sex?"

"That depends on several factors." The doctor stripped her glasses off of her face and put on a serious expression. "Tell me what happened to you last night."

Dixie pressed her thumb and forefinger against the bridge of her nose to stem the tears. "I think someone slipped me a mickey, but I'm not sure what happened. He says we did, but I'm not convinced." She relayed her suspicions.

"Come on." Dr. Khan stood and took her hand. "Let's go check."

***

The combination of pain killers and booze had Dan three sheets to the wind before lunch time. He was about to ask for assistance to his room when a somewhat familiar face entered the bar.

Dan's spine stiffened, and he sobered a little as the beaver and three biggish men sat at a table in a corner.

What in the world was Eddie the Bookie doing in Las Vegas?

Dan wanted to go to his room and sleep off his chemically induced stupor, but his chivalry wouldn't allow it. He needed to be sure Dixie was safe.

"Hey, Travis," he called to the bartender. "You got a phone back there I can use real quick?"

"Sure thing, Big Dan." Travis, a Native American with long black hair, placed a phone on the bar.

Dan dialed Dixie's room but got no answer. He dialed the front desk to make sure she hadn't checked out. It would be just like her to run away—the treacherous witch. He shouldn't care what happened to her, but as much as he wanted to, he couldn't turn off the love valve on his stupid heart so easily.

Next, he dialed Ron's room.

"Hello?" a female voice answered.

The music in the background competed with

the laughter of more than one woman.

"Dixie, please." Dan kept his tone short and clipped.

"Is there a Dixie here?" the woman shouted.

"Give it to me. Ron Flint here." His words slurred, clearly intoxicated. "Dixie, is that you? We're having a party, and it would be *so* much better if you were here. I would give you some more of the stuff that knocked your ass out last night, but I'm not into necrophilia, and you were like a corpse. I couldn't get it up even with your perfect naked body lying there, ripe for the picking."

His chuckle sounded distant then grew louder. "Damn you, get up here, and I'll show you what you missed last night."

"I'll be right there." Dan gently placed the phone down and roughly gathered his wooden walking aids.

The son of a bitch was gonna pay. Dixie hadn't slept with Ron, but the bastard had drugged her with hopes that she would. Dan would kill him with his bare hands…or one of his blasted crutches.

On second thought, he paused and asked for a pen and paper. He jotted down the phone numbers for Southland and Nancy then gave them to Travis. "If you see the cops hauling my ass out of here, call these folks for me."

"Wait a minute, Big Dan. If you need some help," he gestured to the crutches, "I know people. Let's just say I have a tribe, and we stick together."

Dan was glad he had Native American roots and had shared his ancestry with the barkeep. It also paid to be a friendly Southern man and a big tipper.

Dan eyed the group at the corner table as one side of his mouth turned up. "Now that you mention it, I could use a little help."

Chapter Thirty-four

Dixie pounded her fist against the hotel room door. When it opened, a red-haired lady in a see-through negligée stood there with a hand on her hip.

Pushing past the woman, Dixie charged in. "It didn't take you long to find a replacement for me, did it, Ron?"

There were three females in the room, all with various shades of red hair. But on the naked one, the carpet clearly didn't match the curtains.

"You're here," Ron said, fully-lit. "Come here and get me off woman. You owe me."

"I'll get something off all right." She meant to find a knife and castrate the man.

Strong hands gripped her from behind, and crutches fell to the floor at her feet.

"Hold on, darlin'. Let the sum bitch explain himself." Dan then addressed Ron, "It better be good, or I'll tear your arms from their sockets."

Ron scrambled out of the bed and covered up

his beans and frank with his hands. "Yeah, I can explain."

"All right, go ahead and tell me why you let me think we had sex last night." Dixie's voice pitched as high as that of a frightened child. "Why did you drug me and take my clothes off, so it looked like we had?"

Dan's arms tightened around her, and she pulled at them, struggling to breathe.

"I thought it was my only shot. Maybe if you thought we'd already done the nasty, you'd do it again out of guilt or desperation or something." A slow smirk formed on Ron's formerly handsome face. "It could've been great, you know?"

Dixie freed one of her hands and fisted it. "Yeah, and how do you think I would feel about group sex? You must be out of your damn mind."

"I told you." Ron gestured to the ladies of the night who were working in broad daylight. "Didn't I warn you Vegas is a crazy good time?"

"Come on, darlin'." Dan pulled her toward the door. "Let's leave this loser to his fun and games. We have more serious matters to discuss."

It was then Dixie noticed Dr. Khan pick up the crutches and give them to Dan. There was a young man there too, tall with long dark hair.

Dixie's face warmed, embarrassed there had been witnesses to her insignificant tirade against a man whose ego was bigger than his situation called for.

After a private meeting in Dan's room, which had her pulse running like a racehorse, Dixie strode into the bar and took a seat. She asked the bartender, Travis, for a soda water.

She hadn't been there three minutes before Eddie approached with his wannabe mustache and velour suit.

"Fancy seeing you here." He turned the toothpick over in his mouth without assistance from his hands.

"Eddie." She tried to sound surprised. "I'm here for a conference. What are you doing in Vegas?"

"Gambling. What else is there?" The black spot between his front teeth drew her attention more strongly than it had before.

"Medical conferences, apparently." She took a small sip of the seltzer Travis placed in front of her. "How've you been?"

"Good, except for one small problem. I had a visit from a PI not long ago. He asked me about you. Imagine my shock when a former police officer, however inexperienced he was, came calling."

"Really? Did he say who hired him?" She clenched her teeth, anger at Dan searing through her.

"Nope, not a clue. But I figured someone had been running her mouth." He pressed his finger against her lips so hard her head was forced backward.

"Miss, is this gentleman bothering you?" Travis asked.

Dixie shifted in her seat and faked a smile. "No, not at all." She returned her attention to the beaver-like man. "Eddie, maybe we should take this conversation to a more private place."

"You're smarter than I gave you credit for, you bimbo." He added the last part after Travis moved away.

He gripped her arm too tightly as he threw a few ones on the bar and dragged her from the room. When the elevator door opened, Dan was standing in the car wearing a bellman's uniform.

Dixie bit the inside of her cheek, so she wouldn't laugh.

"Going up?" Dan asked, eyeballing Eddie's grip on Dixie's bare arm.

Where he got a hotel uniform to fit him, she'd never know. He moved to the side as Dixie, Eddie, and his three goons entered the small space.

"Five," Eddie said.

At the same time he pressed the button for the floor, Dan grabbed the walkie-talkie on his pocket and said, "Five."

"You must be some dignitary to have so many bodyguards." Dan spoke with no trace of a Southern accent.

"It's helps to know people," Eddie said.

"Yeah, it does." Dan cleared his throat. "Helps to have friends in low places."

Dixie made her eyes focus on the floor. Looking at Dan might endanger him. And though she could shake the snot out of him, she loved him too much to see him get hurt.

"What's the matter, bimbo?" Eddie squeezed her arm to the point she nearly cried out. "Not ready to face the consequences of your big mouth?"

Instead of yelling, she clenched her teeth and

shut her eyes. "I never said anything, Eddie. I swear."

"Even after your little house fire?"

"You burned down my house? You son of a bitch." She reared back and slapped the piss out of him.

He let her go and stumbled into one of his guys, causing another one to grab her by both arms.

"Security, domestic disturbance on five," Dan said into his walkie-talkie as the elevator door opened.

"There's no need for that, mister." Eddie held his cheek as he stepped off the elevator.

***

Dan moved as fast as he could on one leg and two sticks of wood. With three big guys and a shrimp named Eddie, Dan was sure he could take them. Confidence was nine-tenths of the law.

As the room door closed, he stuck one of his crutches in the space, put his shoulder into it, and pushed his way inside.

He dropped one crutch and swung the other at dipshit number one. Blood and teeth hit the floor before the guy's head did. Goon number two was quick and tackled Dan.

He got the crutch up in time to simultaneously catch the man in the nads and under the chin. The heavy man rolled off of him, both hands cradling his injuries.

With little success, Dan struggled to get to his foot.

"Get him," Eddie said.

Dixie leapt onto Eddie's back and sank her

teeth into the soft flesh of the weasel's neck.

"Freaking bloodsucker." Eddie tried to sling her off, but if there was one thing Dan knew, his woman could ride a bucking bronc.

About the time goon number three grabbed for Dan's collar, the door burst open, and Travis along with two other long-haired fellas came in to take out the bad guys.

"Dan." Dixie knelt at his side. "Are you okay, sweetheart?" She pushed his hair back and held his face as she examined his eyes.

"You do love me, don't you?" His voice trembled with the effort of holding himself up.

"Of course I do, you stupid jerk. I love you with all my heart." She kissed him hard.

"I'm sorry I never told you, but I love you too." He reached into his pocket and fell back onto the floor, wincing from the pain in his hip as he held up the little black box. "Please put me out of my misery and say you'll marry me."

After a moment of no sound, he opened his eyes and lifted his head to see her staring open-mouthed at the treasure in his hand.

Her response came out as stubborn as the woman who spoke the words. "If you promise to take care of yourself, I promise to marry you."

"Good," he said as his head fell back onto the carpeted floor. "Did you sign the papers?"

"What papers?"

He laughed, a weak sound. "Nevermind." He lifted a hand. "Help me up so we can go get hitched."

"How 'bout we sleep on it," she said. "I don't

even have a dress yet."

"Excuse me," Travis said as the cops cuffed and hauled the goons out of the room. "My cousins have a chapel nearby. You can borrow an old blue dress from there. That takes care of three traditions. I'm guessing the ring is new, so that covers everything."

Dan looked hopefully at Dixie.

"Let's get this man up, so I can marry him."

Dan smiled through the pain. True joy was a powerful motivator.

Epilogue

Dixie held on to Dan as she pledged her heart and life to him. He refused to use his crutches, so Dixie was on the edges of her two-inch heels in case she needed to support him.

There was one witness present who no one could see, except Dixie. Ella Baker smiled and nodded before she disappeared in a flash of white light.

"Darlin'," he interrupted the officiant, "you're making me nervous."

"I'm sorry, but I don't like you on your own two feet." She stepped closer to tighten her grip on his arm.

His smile warmed her heart.

"I think you need to get me to the honeymoon suite quick." Dan glanced down the aisle from where she'd come.

"You have to say 'I do' and kiss the bride first. Right, Indian Elvis?" Dixie bit her lip as she fixed

Fool With My Heart

her eyes on Travis' cousin who'd introduced himself by the name she'd just used.

"I'm all shook up." The man flipped his long dark hair over the shoulder of his white rhinestone-studded suit.

"Okay, I do," Dan said. "I promise to love you forever, Dixie. Where do I sign, brother?"

***

Back at the room, Dan begged her to help him out of his clothes as fast as she had the first night, but she took her sweet time. Their first experience had been a rush job. This would be different.

"I'm not sure our union is legal, Big Dan." She unbuttoned his shirt anyway.

"It's legal. I'm not under the influence of very many drugs at the moment."

"Uh, Dan." She smacked his chest. "How am I supposed to take you seriously when you keep messing with me?"

He covered her hand with his. "Come here, darlin'." He pulled her down until her head rested on his chest. "I love messing with you, and I'm gonna do it forever."

She raised her chin until their lips were close. "Lucky me."

"I don't think you knew you were ready to marry me, but you did it anyway."

"I was ready." She brushed her fingertips along his jawline as she looked into his eyes. "My heart's at home with you."

"Mine too, darlin'." He kissed her. "I hope you don't mind having to do most of the work on this makeshift honeymoon. I'll make it up to you later."

"It's no chore, and I know you'll do your part when you can." She winked and kissed her way down to his bellybutton.

When he shuddered, she grinned up at him from beneath lush lashes.

Dixie Baker had his number and his heart.

***

When they returned to Southland, they found that Aunt May, Uncle Ben Hill, and Nancy had helped the kids put together a wedding party.

Dan was relieved to hear the adults had discussed his irrational orders and decided not to take action until he and Dixie had a chance to work things out.

The legal papers were still in Dixie's bag when they got home. They both gladly signed the adoption papers, but he tore the prenuptial papers to bits.

Then Dan led his bride to the barn to give her the first of many wedding presents.

"Mrs. Baker," he removed the blue bandanna blindfold from her eyes, "meet Sugarfoot. He's all yours, darlin'."

She hugged the horse and wiped her leaky eyes. "You're everything I ever wanted."

"Glad I could provide," Dan said.

"I'm talking about you, love-of-mine." She turned to face him. "Come here, you handsome devil."

He wrapped his arms around her and leaned into her kiss.

"Whew. I love you too, darlin'." He fanned himself. "You know, it was a real frog strangler last night. I think the Blazer's screaming for us to make another attempt to get stuck in the mud."

She reached behind her back, unhooked her bra, and slid the straps down her shoulders. Then she tossed the thing up into the hayloft, which left her in nothing but a tank top and cutoff jeans.

"Let's go, Big D."

ABOUT THE AUTHOR

Meda White is an award-winning author who writes sweet, sultry, and southern contemporary and new adult romance. Born with Georgia clay running through her veins, she continues to enjoy the Southern lifestyle with her husband, a very spoiled Collie, and a stray cat who adopted the family. When not writing, you might find her making music, shooting zombie targets, teaching yoga, or explaining the meaning of her unusual first name.

A Note to Readers

Dear Reader,

Thank you for reading *Home With My Heart*. I hope you enjoyed Dan and Dixie's love story.

If you're interested in the other Southland Romances, turn the page for a sneak peek at *Play With My Heart* to see Liz all grown up.

If you have a moment to leave an honest review, I'd really appreciate it. Not only do reviews let authors know how they're doing, they help readers find new books.

I love to hear from readers. Please look for me on my Website, Facebook, Twitter, and my Dirt Road Darlings street team. If you sign up for my Newsletter, which contains bonus material and sometimes prizes, it'll make sure you never miss a new release.

Thank you, and best wishes for a lifetime of love and laughter. Oh, and don't forget to get stuck in the mud every now and then.

Meda

Play With My Heart
A Southland Romance, Book 1

Liz Baker aimed her front kick at the middle of the wooden spindle and smiled when it detached, flying several feet to land on her brother's landscaped lawn. "This is so much fun. Thanks for inviting me to come for a visit and help replace your deck."

"Yeah, I can tell you like to kick stuff. You're not thinking of a certain man while you're doing that are you?" Danny stood off to the side, but splinters still flew too close to his head.

"No, I'm way past…him." Her ex-husband's handsome face flashed in her mind. She took out two slats at one time and pumped her fist in triumph.

Danny raised a brow. "Hmm. So you're ready to move on?"

"I didn't say that." Liz aimed another sidekick at a skinny piece of wood. "I may never be ready for that."

The pressure of a barrier slamming down in her mind to trap the hurt inside felt real. Compartmentalizing was a coping mechanism. Her ex-husband had broken her heart in a bad way. As a result, she spent the three years following Jason's betrayal concentrating on her career. Her hard work paid off, but about the time she considered moving on, he came back into her life.

Liz wasn't dumb enough to take him back, but he wasn't looking for that. What he offered her was an explanation and a dream come true. They were amateur musicians who spent their youth writing terrible songs and plotting to put a band together. Once or twice a month, Liz got onstage at a little country bar near Atlanta to play her guitar and sing with her ex-husband and the band. She suffered no delusions that she was the next American Idol (she was too old for that anyway), but she loved to get lost in the music.

Music, its ability to move your soul, was something her biological father shared with her before his death. She was young, but it stuck with her through the years. Playing her guitar was a safe way to express the emotions she intellectualized the majority of the time.

Movement out of the corner of her eye from the house located behind her brother's home caught her attention. She looked up and saw a man watching her from his own back door. She turned to tell Danny, but he'd just gone inside carrying the outdoor dining table over his head. Turning back toward the stranger, she noted he filled the frame of the doorway. And it was the full sliding glass kind. Other than his size, she couldn't tell much about him…except that he might be blond.

She hoped he wouldn't call the cops. From his perspective, she might look like a woman hell bent on revenge by demolishing Danny's deck. She supposed her brother's Los Angeles neighbors didn't get to see many Southern women unleashed.

Also Available from Meda White

Play With My Heart
A Southland Romance, Book 1

Southern musician and closet geek Liz Baker enjoys her quiet life. While in Los Angeles helping her brother with a house project, the simple life gets complicated when British television actor Ian Clarke walks into the picture.

Ian enjoys his celebrity status in Hollywood and is determined nothing and no one will get in the way of his plans for success on the big screen. He never counted on meeting a woman like Liz, but she's the only one who can help him with a personal problem.

Forced into close quarters where priorities and cultures clash, an intense attraction catches them both by surprise. Secrets, old lovers, and the paparazzi threaten their new dreams and a chance for love could be lost forever.

***Play With My Heart* won the 2014 BTS Red Carpet Award in Contemporary Romance.**

Additional books in the series:

Dance With My Heart: A Southland Romance, Book 2

Ride With My Heart: A Southland Romance, Book 3

Fool With My Heart: A Southland Romance, Book 4

Home With My Heart: A Southland Romance-The Prequel

Christmas Give
A Holiday Novella

Eva Walker returns home to Georgia for the first Christmas since her husband's death. She's missed her family, but is afraid the void left by her husband will make it unbearable.

Between losing his job as an NFL defensive back and losing his wife to the star quarterback, Adam "Mack" Riggs has had a rough year. Looking for a change of pace, he visits an old college friend for Christmas.

The attraction between Eva and Adam is instant, and so is the laughter. Enjoying life again feels so good for both of them. Simple Christmas wishes unite with a shared holiday tradition, putting them on a path toward healing and acceptance. A path that could lead to a future, if only their pasts would remain where they belong.

The Southern College Novellas

Spring Fling
A Southern College Novella

Kellyn Crenshaw wants to make it to college graduation without becoming another notch on the belt of a fraternity boy. A boy exactly like Pace Samson. Forced into close proximity because their roommates are dating, Kellyn sets out to prove she's resistant to his charms.

Pace never figured himself for a one-woman man until he spends time with Kellyn. She's different, and he can't get her out of his mind. She's also aware of his reputation, and it may keep him from the one girl who makes him want to change his ways.

When Pace and Kellyn fake a fling on Spring Break to help their friends, Kellyn may discover she isn't immune to Pace after all. They'll each have to decide if what's between them is just a fling or if there's a chance their feelings are real.

Fall Rush
A Southern College Novella

Embry Harris is desperate to turn things around her senior year of college. She's determined to make more responsible choices and rid herself of the stigma plaguing her. But because of her job and the hot bartender who goads her into making impulsive decisions, it isn't going to be easy.

Stede Bennett's mission since returning from his overseas tour is to get his degree. The last thing he needs is a spoiled sorority girl distracting him. Being a Marine taught him many things, except how to handle a beautiful woman in constant need of saving.

Protecting Embry from the jerk threatening to ruin her reputation is how Stede begins to lose his heart. Being empowered by Stede's words is how Embry starts losing hers. If the schemer responsible for pushing them together gets his way, they could lose their chance for happiness.

Winter Formal
A Southern College Novella

Life is going according to plan for Sibba Douglas until she gets blackmailed. Her future dream of being a doctor is threatened unless she can help a spoiled fraternity boy do well on the MCAT.

Nash Lincoln knows he needs to settle down and focus on his studies, but academics have taken a back seat to social events, and he's coasting by on little sleep and lots of pills. The distraction of a tutor he's admired from afar isn't helping matters.

Substance abuse leads to tragedy and draws Sibba and Nash closer together. But it may also be the thing that tears them apart.

Made in United States
Orlando, FL
03 May 2022